The Bomb-itty of Errors

Written by
Jordan Allen-Dutton,
Jason Catalano,
Gregory J. Qaiyum,
and Erik Weiner

Music by
Jeffrey Qaiyum

A SAMUEL FRENCH ACTING EDITION

NEW YORK HOLLYWOOD LONDON TORONTO

SAMUELFRENCH.COM

Copyright © 2010 by Jordan Allen-Dutton, Jason Catalano,
Gregory J. Qaiyum, and Erik Weiner

ALL RIGHTS RESERVED

CAUTION: Professionals and amateurs are hereby warned that *THE BOMB-ITTY OF ERRORS* is subject to a Licensing Fee. It is fully protected under the copyright laws of the United States of America, the British Commonwealth, including Canada, and all other countries of the Copyright Union. All rights, including professional, amateur, motion picture, recitation, lecturing, public reading, radio broadcasting, television and the rights of translation into foreign languages are strictly reserved. In its present form the play is dedicated to the reading public only.

The amateur live stage performance rights to *THE BOMB-ITTY OF ERRORS* are controlled exclusively by Samuel French, Inc., and licensing arrangements and performance licenses must be secured well in advance of presentation. PLEASE NOTE that amateur Licensing Fees are set upon application in accordance with your producing circumstances. When applying for a licensing quotation and a performance license please give us the number of performances intended, dates of production, your seating capacity and admission fee. Licensing Fees are payable one week before the opening performance of the play to Samuel French, Inc., at 45 W. 25th Street, New York, NY 10010.

Licensing Fee of the required amount must be paid whether the play is presented for charity or gain and whether or not admission is charged.

Stock licensing fees quoted upon application to Samuel French, Inc.

For all other rights than those stipulated above, visit *THE BOMB-ITTY OF ERRORS* website at www.bomb-itty.com.

Particular emphasis is laid on the question of amateur or professional readings, permission and terms for which must be secured in writing from Samuel French, Inc.

Copying from this book in whole or in part is strictly forbidden by law, and the right of performance is not transferable.

Whenever the play is produced the following notice must appear on all programs, printing and advertising for the play: "Produced by special arrangement with Samuel French, Inc."

Due authorship credit must be given on all programs, printing and advertising for the play.

ISBN 978-0-573-69844-6   Printed in U.S.A.   #29639

No one shall commit or authorize any act or omission by which the copyright of, or the right to copyright, this play may be impaired.

No one shall make any changes in this play for the purpose of production.

Publication of this play does not imply availability for performance. Both amateurs and professionals considering a production are strongly advised in their own interests to apply to Samuel French, Inc., for written permission before starting rehearsals, advertising, or booking a theatre.

No part of this book may be reproduced, stored in a retrieval system, or transmitted in any form, by any means, now known or yet to be invented, including mechanical, electronic, photocopying, recording, videotaping, or otherwise, without the prior written permission of the publisher.

OPTIONAL RENTAL MATERIALS

Three CDs consisting of **Instrumental Backing Tracks and 'Scratch'/Sample Tracks** will be loaned two months prior to the production ONLY on the receipt of the Licensing Fee quoted for all performances and the rental fee.

Please contact Samuel French for perusal of the music materials as well as a performance license application.

Please note that these CDs are not mandatory and that producing companies are welcome to create their own backing tracks.

IMPORTANT BILLING AND CREDIT REQUIREMENTS

All producers of *THE BOMB-ITTY OF ERRORS must* give credit to the Author of the Play in all programs distributed in connection with performances of the Play, and in all instances in which the title of the Play appears for the purposes of advertising, publicizing or otherwise exploiting the Play and/or a production. The name of the Author *must* appear on a separate line on which no other name appears, immediately following the title and *must* appear in size of type not less than fifty percent of the size of the title type.

THE BOMB-ITTY OF ERRORS was first produced by Daryl Roth, Michael Lynne, Q Brothers and Hal Luftig at 45 Bleecker Street Theatre in New York City on December 12, 1999. The sets were by Scott Pask, costumes by David C. Woolard, lighting by James Vermeulen, sound by One Dream Sound and Sunil Rajan, the production Stage Manager was Kate Broderick. The cast was as follows:

ANTIPHOLUS OF SYRACUSE/
   MC HENDELBERG/ABBESS . . . . Gregory J. Qaiyum
DROMIO OF EPHESUS/LUCIANA/COP . . . . Erik Weiner
DROMIO OF SYRACUSE/DR. PINCH/DESI . . . . Jason Catalano
ANTIPHOLUS OF EPHESUS/
   ADRIANA/BOBBY . . . . Jordan Allen-Dutton
DJ . . . . Jeffrey Qaiyum

THE BOMB-ITTY OF ERRORS was originally Developed and Directed by Andrew Goldberg.

CHARACTERS

ACTOR 1 – Dromio of Syracuse, Desi, Dr. Pinch, Backup singer, Hendelberg Double #4

ACTOR 2 – Antipholus of Ephesus, Adriana, Bobby, Backup singer, Receive Cat, Hendelberg Double #2

ACTOR 3 – Antipholus of Syracuse, Hendelberg, Abbess, Luciana Double

ACTOR 4 – Dromio of Ephesus, Luciana, Cop, C-Fake, Felicio, Shakespeare

AUTHORS' NOTES

Just as Shakespeare's work is malleable and open to interpretation and re-imagination, so is *The Bomb-itty of Errors*.

All productions of *The Bomb-itty of Errors* have included a DJ onstage that interacts with the characters and the audience. Obviously, the music is an integral part of the show. We've noted where the beats come in and out. It may be possible to do the show without a DJ and have a sound person in a booth playing the tracks, but it will undoubtedly play better with a person live onstage.

A note about the optional backing CDs, available from Samuel French: rented music will come on three CDs. Two CDs will be identical - those are the Instrumentals. The third CD is a Scratch Track that includes someone rapping over the Instrumentals to show how and where the lyrics fit - this is for listening/rehearsal purposes only. In some cases, the lyrics on the Scratch Track may differ from the script. Please use the script as the ultimate authority on lyrics. The two instrumental CDs are for the DJ for the performances - ideally the DJ would have two CD players and a mixer to cut between the two CDs - this way the DJ can cue up the next music cue and cut between tracks. We've also included extra time at the end of every Instrumental - this is in case the actors fall off rhythm, they won't have to worry about the song ending abruptly and can take a beat before getting back on rhythm.

To obtain the tracks please contact Samuel French through their website at SamuelFrench.com.

Some productions have stuck closely to having only four actors, as in the original production. Other productions have cast many actors in the different roles.

We have included notes and stage directions from the original production. Feel free to use them or create your own.

We have also included some alternate lyrics (page 90) if you would like to have some "cleaner" lyrics for younger or more sensitive audiences. Alternate lyrics are available if a line has a endnote beside it that indicates it's placement in the appendix.

We hope you enjoy performing, directing, and working on *The Bomb-itty of Errors* and get caught up in the fun and electric energy of the show.

All the best,
The Bomb-itty Crew

ACT 1

Prologue

(The prologue is performed by the 4 actors, dressed in contemporary hip-hop gear. The numbers [1-4] in the prologue refer to assigned lines by actor in the original production. Feel free to use this division or create your own.)

1. Thirty years ago...
ALL. ...in New York City
This bitty named Betty that was oh so pretty
Met an M.C. by the name of M.C. Egeon
Who could get 'em jumpin' no matter what stage he's on
M.C. Ege would grab the mic and...
4. ...rock it
Take the crowd, pull 'em in, and...
2. ...stick 'em in his pocket
ALL. Nobody could
3. knock it
ALL. he was an
1. innovator
ALL. In a freestyle match, you never
1. had a prayer
3. He was a metaphor for hip-hop in its early stages
1 & 2. *(BEAT #1 STARTS)* A true art form that would last for ages
4. Now M.C. Egeon and Betty got locked up
1, 2, & 3. Married, that is
4. Then Betty got knocked up

1, 2, & 3. Pregnant, that is,
4. and her stomach started growin'
Bigger and bigger until she was overblowin'
2. M.C. E was flowin', workin' the rap circuit
Talkin' with his agents, startin' to network it
Tryin' to make the bank to secure his kid's future
Buyin' new dresses for Betty that would suit her
1. 'Cause she was growin'
1 & 4. larger
1. and
1 & 4. wider every minute
1. Looking down at her tummy wondering,
ALL. "What's in it?"
1. Four months later in a downtown hospital
Betty gave birth to what was then impossible:
ALL. Quadruplets –
3. four baby boys
I'm talkin' four –
ALL. what? –
3. beautiful bundles of joy
Now M.C. E had been preparing financially
For one little kid so when they came out sequentially
ALL. 1 to the 2 the 3 the 4
His heart skipped a beat and he almost hit the floor
4. There were two sets of identical twins all at once
Two big healthy boys and two little runts
3. Now M.C. E had never been good at choosin' names
So without much thought he named two pairs the same
4. One he named
3. Antipholus,
4. the other
1. Dromio
4. The next he named

2. Antipholus
1. and then another
4. Dromio
2. In the next few years times were very
ALL. rough
2. When it came down to money
ALL. E never had enough
1. Four times as many cradles
3. and four pacifiers
4. Four times as many bottles
2. and mounds of dirty diapers
4. Ya'see M.C. E was losin' it, his bank account was
1, 2, & 3. tapped
4. And a negative vibe flowed inside every
1, 2, & 3. rap
4. His vocab was all
1, 2, & 3. sapped
4. and his concerts always
1, 2, & 3. stunk
4. He didn't have the energy to
ALL. resurrect the funk
2 & 4. So he started sellin' skunk,
2 & 3. you know, cheeba,
1. weed?[1]
2. Just to try and get by and give his family what they need
ALL. He took heed
2. to sell it only to the heads he trusted
But it wasn't too long before M.C. E got
1 & 2. busted
1. Locked up, that is, in a local penitentiary
Leaving Betty alone with the boys unintentionally
ALL. Essentially
1. the family was in a state of crisis

     Dead broke and burdened by the system's many vices
ALL. The choices:
1.   to try to survive and pray for sanity
3. Or offer up the children to a foster family
     They opted for the latter and with sadness and bravery
2 & 3. Betty drove the kids to the adoption agency
4. Now M.C. E's
1, 2, & 3.   rap style
4.   was changing while
1, 2, & 3.   in prison
4. A frightened less
1, 2, & 3.   enlightened
4.   vision had
1, 2, & 3.   arisen
ALL. His decision to give away his children had undone him
3. And the guilt inside and swallowed pride had overrun him
4. One day in his cell he put his head down and
1, 2, & 3.   cried
4. Dropped a pill of
1, 2, & 3.   cyanide
4.   and committed
1, 2, & 3.   suicide
4. Betty learned
1, 2, & 3.   that he'd died
4.   the very next day
     And as tragedy would have it, she died the same way
2. Meanwhile, the children at the tender age of two
     Were separated from each other
ALL.   – sad but true
4. One Dromio
2.   and one Antipholus
3, 4. Were brought up in the fine city of Ephesus

1, 2. Too young to understand and too young to choose
   The other two were raised in the town of Syracuse
4. And as the brothers grew up on opposite coasts
2. One night they were visited by their father's ghost
1. And he told his sons of their hip-hop history
3. And said in a voice that was filled with mystery,
4. "One day you will find your missing link
   When you look in the mirror and you see yourself blink…"
1. Blink.
3.   Blink.
2.   Blink.
ALL.   Hoo-Ha!
4. The ghost disappeared
2.   and their life proceeded
1. And each young man
3.   made a vow that they needed
1. To live up to their father's M.C. legacy
   To be the best M.C. the world would ever see
2. The two Antipholi,
3.   the bigger of the family
2. Made the smaller Dromios
2 & 3.   be their back-up M.C.s
1 & 4. And so it was the Dromios were treated like crap crap
   Having to sing back-up on Antipholus' rap rap
3. They grew up livin' in a world of hip-hop
2. Surrounded by the
ALL.   "1, 2,"
4.   surrounded by the
ALL.   "1, 2"
1.   surrounded by the
ALL.   "1, 2, 3" and "You don't [**BEAT:***stop!*]"

(BEAT #1 STOPS)

4. Thus ends the prologue and comes the beginnin'
ALL. So welcome to a new world that ya never been in……
Enough rough stuff to make your mind start spinnin'
Listen up close so you can grab an earful
Some parts'll make you cheerful and some'll make you tearful
Don't be fearful, y'all, it's no drama, see

1. Is it a tragedy? –
ALL. NO! –
1. Is it a comedy? –
ALL. WELL…

It's a new style, it's whatever we wanna be
So welcome, welcome, welcome to the Bomb-itty!
Go…………

(BEAT #2 STARTS)

Dromio,
Go, Dromio, go, go, go Dromio,
Go, Dromio, Go, Dromio, go, go, go, Dromio,
(1 & 2 exit.)
Go, Dromio, Go, Dromio, go, go, go, Dromio
Go, Dromio, Go, Dromio, go, go, go, Drom-I-O!

Scene One
The Mart

*(Enter **ANTIPHOLUS OF SYRACUSE (A.S.)** and **DROMIO OF SYRACUSE (D.S.)**. They both hold large bags from their travels. Dromio wears a child's backpack and carries a colorful kid's recorder and microphone.)*

BOTH. Yo, we're on a mission – everybody listen
    We're representing Syracuse and we're never quittin'
A.S. Well if your name is Dromio then give me a sign
D.S. If your name's Antipholus then bust me a rhyme
A.S. It's that time
D.S.   again for the fun to
A.S.   begin
    For the fun to
D.S.   begin it's that time
A.S.   once again
    It's time to freak freak, it's time to get busy
D.S. The beats are so sweet, the rhymes'll make you dizzy
A.S. As we flyin' in we gettin' higher than[2]
    The highest string on the violin
D.S. Antipholus, Dromio, there's no stoppin' this
    Rockin', hip-hoppin' each and every metropolis
A.S. Yo livin' on the road, we never expected this
D.S. Where we at now, brother?
A.S.   Ephesus, Ephesus
D.S. Live and direct from the town next to this
A.S. What's the most important meal?
D.S.   Breakfast is, breakfast is
A.S. You and me, we be like beat poets
D.S. Travellin' the world on and on the go it's
A.S. In and outta in and outta in and outta
D.S.   States
    We be lookin' for the meaning of the missing link

A.S. Phrase **(BEAT #2 STOPS)**
BOTH. So once more, we'll say it loud
   As we move through the city we move the crowd
   (BEAT #3 STARTS) 'Cause we're on a mission – everybody listen
   We're representing Syracuse and we're never quittin'
A.S. So Dromio
D.S. Yeah?
A.S. Go Dromio
D.S. Where?
A.S. And take these thousand marks of gold

(**ANTIPHOLUS** *tosses* **DROMIO** *a bag of gold.*)

D.S. What you want me to do with all of this cash flow?
A.S. Pay the ho-tel, I mean the mo-tel, I mean the
BOTH. Ephesus Inn
A.S. I'll see you in about one hour, kid, when it be time for my din
D.S. din
A.S. Till then I'll cruise around this town
   Once up the street and then
BOTH. back down
A.S. Word has it this is a phat city
   Where a dog like me
D.S. Woof!
A.S. Can find a little kitty
D.S. Meow!
A.S. I'll give a quick look and then hit the sack
   'Cause after carryin' this pack, jack, I gotta stiff back
D.S. Well, I'm stiff too, bro
A.S. Get outta here, Dro
D.S. Havin' so much dough, I'm good to go so

(**DROMIO** *begins to exit.*)

A.S. A trusty villain, with me he chillin'

(DROMIO runs back on.)

BOTH. What more can I say

A.S. We grillin'
M.C.'s from Ephesus to Syracuse

BOTH. And since you heard the news

D.S. *(singing)* Party people, I'm Drom-io, oh-oh-io,
Oh, io, oh, oh, io,
Oh, io, oh, oh, io,
Come on, everybody, do the baseball

(DROMIO exits.)

A.S. He's always got a little somethin' funny to do
To make the sun rise up when I'm feelin' blue
I been watchin' over this boy since we was two
Me and little bro Dro be the top duo crew
But sometimes I feel beat, I don't know what to think
Will we ever find the meaning of this missing link?
Do you know what it's like to look yourself in the mirror
With vision 20/20 but you can't see clear?
To be kept on a shelf, not seein' what you wanna see,
Not knowin' yourself, bein' half of what you wanna be?
We been on the ground of town after town
But what it is we look for we have not found
So I keep pushin' on through the struggle of life
To one day find the pleasure that'll ease my strife
So I change my mind just like I knew I would
Breathe deep, look around, and know that it's all good
So for now I'll dine, maybe drink some wine
Maybe later do a little of the Bump 'n Grind[3]
Maybe later do a little of the Bump 'n Grind
Maybe later do a little of the Bump – **(BEAT #3 FADES)**

(DROMIO OF EPHESUS (D.E.) enters.)

A.S. – But check it: here's Dromio
Yo, what you returned so soon fo'?

(BEAT #4 STARTS)

D.E. Returned so soon, nay, I find you not in time
For you are committing a domestic crime
The stove is on and the meat is cookin'
The clock struck twelve and I – started lookin'
Your wife struck one across my pate
I receive all your blows 'cause you are late
The food is cold that you should be eating
If you come not home I'll receive another beating
Don't make her think you're cheating, return to your home
So she'll stop hitting me on my dome
I'm Drom – io, oh, oh, io –
Oh, io, oh, oh, io,
Oh, io, oh, oh, io –

(SNAP! **ANTIPHOLUS** *snaps* **DROMIO OF EPHESUS** *in the head.)*

D.E. – Ow, you know, your servant?
See the bump on my head, do I deserve it?

A.S. Stop in your wind sir listen close I pray
Tell me where you've stashed the cash I gave you, okay?

D.E. Oh the five spot that you gave me last week?
To give to the barber who lives down the street?
For the new red wig that you bought your wife?
I gave it to him, sir, and that's on my life

A.S. My present sense of humor is lacking in sport
We're strangers in danger on a course we can't abort
I gave you all our gold because I trusted thee
Now how did such a large charge leave thy custody?

D.E. You can joke around later while you eat your food
For your wife waits up in a bitter mood
If I return with news that you come not to bed
Every word that I speak means a blow to my head
See I'll be dead, sir, if you come not soon
So follow me sir, like the sun follows moon

A.S. Once again friend have done your foolishness
   Tell me where my money is or else, get the jist?
   Are you dismissin' the task that I gave you? Don't you listen?
D.E. My mission lacks suspicion, 'tis but a task
   To fetch you from the market and to bring you home fast
   Alas your wife and her sister both await
   Your return to the house before it's too late
   (BEAT #4 STOPS)
A.S. What wife? None such one exists in my life!
   Don't you remember? I haven't got my groove on since November!
D.E. Your worship's wife, my mistress at the Phoenix
   Who waits at the table, her hands full of Kleenex
   Praying that soon you will be home for dinner
   Even as we stay here the rage grows within her
A.S. You sinner, messin' after what I said
   Here's one for your stomach –

   *(**ANTIPHOLUS** knees **DROMIO**, who falls to his knees.)*

A.S.   – and one for your head

   *(**ANTIPHOLUS** stands in front of **DROMIO** and "slaps" him back and forth as **DROMIO** slaps his own hands to make the sound effect.)*

D.E. What the hell are you doing, for God's sake, peace[4]
   I said please, sir, please, I said peace, sir, peace, etc.

   *(**ANTIPHOLUS** stops slapping **DROMIO** and steps aside. **DROMIO** continues clapping and moving his head as though he is being slapped still. **ANTIPHOLUS** comes behind him and wraps his arm around **DROMIO**'s neck.)*

D.E. But you don't seem to cease,
A.S.   Hell, no![5]
D.E.   so like a pig drenched in grease
   I will fly like the geese to your home in the East

*(**DROMIO OF EPHESUS** elbows **ANTIPHOLUS** and exits.)*

A.S. What the world could this be? He's mad confusin me
Upon my life, by some device or other
I discover this villain whom I call my brother
If I had my 'druthers the facts would be uncovered
They say this city's nuts
They say it takes guts
Just to step inside
Don't always believe what you see in the eyes
Of these passers-by
'Cause on the streets they getting high[6]
You got sorcerers on corners who can slide inside your mind
Sally's in back alleys gettin bucks for they behinds
Cheaters, cons, pranksters, mafiosos
Dealers, guns, gangsters – where did Dro go?
I'm off to the hotel to go seek this knave
And find out what happened to the money I gave

(ANTIPHOLUS OF SYRACUSE *exits.)*

Scene Two
Antipholus of Ephesus' House

(**ADRIANA (ADR)**, *wearing a red wig, and* **LUCIANA (LUC)**, *in blonde wig, enter from Antipholus of Ephesus' house.*)

(BEAT #5 STARTS)

LUC. *(spoken)* I'm hungry, sister

ADR. *(spoken)* Yes, sister, I heard you the first time
Well, neither my husband nor his man has returned
Two hours passed and no knowledge learned
I'm spurned –

LUC. – No wait, sister, I have a hunch
Perhaps Antipholus is just out to lunch
Let's go eat, later we can meet 'em
A man is a master of his own freedom
They come and go as they please
When they feel like eating cheese, they eat cheese
It's been that way since times were ancient
We must go inside, sister, please be patient

ADR. And why should their liberty be more than ours?

LUC. Duh – they work outside and we work indoors

ADR. But if I did this to him he would lose his temper

LUC. That's 'cause in this house he is the largest member

ADR. You would not say so if you were his wife
How comes it he gives me so much strife?

LUC. There is so much unfairness in this life
We are all equal under heaven's eye
But earth has different rules than the holy sky
The beasts, the fishes, the wingèd birds
Are all just slaves to just one word:
Man – divine, master of all these
Lord of the wide world and watery seas
Filled with knowledge, wit, and strength

Big manly muscles of width and length
They are the masters of their wives and mistresses
And we should attend to all of their wisheshes

(pause)

ADR. Oh yeah, well, tell me what if you were wed?
LUC. I would lie in bed and give my husband head – y[7]
Conversation, we would laugh and sigh
And he would rock me to sleep with a long lullaby
ADR. And what if he told you to cook him a feast?
LUC. I would cook up a rack of sparebacks with two beasts
ADR. Well, what if he called you an ugly giraffe?
LUC. I don't know what that is so I'd probably just laugh
ADR. What would you do if your husband came home late?
LUC. I'd stand in the doorway, buttnaked, and wait[8]

*(**LUCIANA** freezes.)* **(MUSIC STOPS)**

ADR. Oh my sweet lord, my sister is crazy
Hard to believe we fell from the same tree
How can she sit there, chastise, and chide
How can she not hear me when I do an aside?

*(**LUCIANA** unfreezes.)* **(MUSIC STARTS)**

ADR. You're a child, one day you'll understand
That a wedded woman's woes are worse than a man's
We bear troubles on our back as we carry the laundry
When walking in public we feel cheap and tawdry
In private they shower us with romance and caresses
But the people with the power wear the pants not the dresses
You're too young, one day you'll see
That a married woman's life is no life to be
LUC. Well, I will marry someday and I will find my Juliet
(BEAT #5 FADES)

*(**LUCIANA** exits.)*

ADR. Juliet? I think she means Romeo
Here comes Dromio!

(DROMIO OF EPHESUS *enters.)*

ADR. Is your master following close behind?

D.E. Now listen, mistress, please be kind
Your husband (**BEAT #6 STARTS**) sends me in his place
His message written on my face

ADR. You waste my time what said you he?

D.E. His fists did speak an hour to me
And as every word on my face did land
I found it much much harder to understand

ADR. Surely you can understand a slap
From your master's hand?

D.E.   – Like a burlap sac
Stuffed with sand his hand did land to reprimand

ALL. *(Offstage)* HOT DAMN!

D.E. Some to my front and some to my end
Impossible to comprehend

ADR. This story bends my ears and lends me fright
Does my husband return home tonight?
He's vowed to vex me every chance that he's had

D.E. Why, mistress, sure my master is horn-mad

ADR. Horn-mad, thou villain?

D.E. (MUSIC STOPS) Wait, wait, wait, wait I said that bad
I didn't mean he's fooling around with other broads
But that his deck is missing all of its cards
When I told him that his supper was getting cold
He asked me for a thousand marks of gold
"Tis time to eat," quoth I; "My money," quoth he
"She cooked meat," quoth I; "'Tis not funny," qouth he
"Return you home?," quoth I; "My gold," he says again
"Where is the thousand marks that I gave thee, villain?"
"I have no mistress, wife, nor maid
It's been seven months since I got laid![9]"

ADR. (MUSIC STARTS) Quoth who?

D.E. Quoth who? My master, who
Who denied straight-face in knowing you
Then straight to my pate, no time to defend

ADR. Hence you mumbling moron, go fetch my husband

D.E. I may mumble, tumble, stumble, trip and fall
All because they all treat me like a soccer ball
Kicked back and forth 'tween husband and a wife
It's a wonder I have lived so long a life
And so I roll back to same juncture
Knowing all too well I will soon puncture **(BEAT #6 STOPS)**

(DROMIO OF EPHESUS exits.)

ADR. My, my what a dreadful account has been spoken
Why, why must a wonderful heart be so broken?
I try but the tears keep on coming, I'm chokin'
I spy with my little eye a man smokin'
And laughing and sighing with another
Woman, a friend, or maybe it's his lover
I'm dying and crying imagining he kissed her
I need someone to hold me...sister!

(LUCIANA enters.)

LUC. There's some weird people dressed in black with headsets back here...

ADR. (BEAT #7 STARTS) I need you, sister

LUC. – I'm here for you

ADR. I love you, sister

LUC. – I shed a tear for you

ADR. I feel so ashamed

LUC. – What's it about, girl?

ADR. He's the one to blame

LUC. – Spell it on out, girl

ADR. While I wait up reading gourmet cook books
My homely duties have stolen my good looks
My once perky body, he was wasted it

LUC. The fruits of your labor only he has tasted it
ADR. But he's eating elsewhere and no doubt he's blowing off
Me and my wonderful meatloaf stroganoff
LUC. But sister, you're such a hot momma
Sister, just give up the ill na–na[10]
ADR. But sister, did you hear what I said
And sister, I'd rather be dead
Than living this lie, forcing these smiles
Why did I ever walk down the aisle?
LUC. But sister, to serve is our duty
And sister, you're totally a cutie
ADR. But sister, I'm still very young
And sister, the jury is hung
And my husband's not and I'm starting to cry[11]
My heart's locked in a vault and I'll tell you why
'Cause it's his own fault
LUC.   – that your bedroom is quiet
ADR. It's his own fault
LUC.   – that you went on that diet
ADR. It's his own fault
LUC.   – that we don't understand space
ADR. It's his own damn fault, I should say it to his face
What ruins are in me, that you have not ruined?
With one nice word our love could be renewed
LUC. But, sister, he promised you a necklace and you will wear it
Around town and show off your twenty four carat
Big gold chain, you can wear it with pride
ADR. It's not the gold that matters but what's inside
If only he'd stay true to his marriage vows
He'd see that the jewel that is best endowed
Is now scowled at
LUC.   – yet he buys you gold!

ADR. Think'st he that I can be so bought and sold
    Hell no, sister[12]
LUC.   but we should put our feelings on hold
    For gold sister,
ADR.   It's time he gets told
    It's his own fault
LUC.   – that you put on some weight
ADR. It's his own fault
LUC.   – that your abs aren't that great
ADR. It's his own fault
LUC.   – that your boobies are swayin'[13]
ADR. It's his own damn fault and it's time I complain
    I'm married to a man with no sense of romance
    What I wouldn't do for some foreplay or a slowdance

ADR. So, listen up, girls, if your hearts feeling tossed
    There's a reason, love labour's are lost
    Husbands don't notice their hot and needy wives
    They spend their nights taking shots in seedy dives
    So I say to those women whose husbands are here
    If he can't start the car, or he's stuck in first gear
    Or he puts you third behind beer and his career
    Let yourself go and scream in his ear

L/A. It's your own fault
ADR.   – that you can't pitch a tent
L/A. It's your own fault
ADR.   – yeah, you know what I meant
L/A. It's your own fault
LUC.   – listen up, all of you gents
L/A. It's your own damn fault and our patience is spent
    If you come home late with no alibi
    Better look us straight in the eye
    And say that you love us and we're still fly
    With tears of joy we will both cry

    (**LUCIANA** and **ADRIANA** *mime spinning records.*)

LUC. We will we will we will we will both cry
ADR. Wiggity wiggity wiggity we will both cry
LUC. Wucka wucka wucka we will both cry
ADR. Chicka wocka wocka we will both cry
LUC. But sister…
ADR.   But sister…
   (ADRIANA exits.)
LUC. Oh, you got a big ol' butt, sister…
   (LUCIANA exits.) **(BEAT #7 FADES)**

Scene Three
The Mart

(**ANTIPHOLUS OF SYRACUSE** *enters.*)

A.S. The dough I gave to Dromio is back at the inn
Why he always got a joke, yo what's wrong with him
According to the hotel concierge
He seeks me out just about everywhere
I could not speak with homie Dromio
Since the worm slipped away from me

(**DROMIO OF SYRACUSE** *enters.*)

A.S. – But what d'ya know?
D.S. If your name's Antipholus then drop me a jewel
A.S. A jewel?

(*SNAP!* **ANTIPHOLUS** *snaps* **DROMIO**'s *head.*)

A.S. I should drop you fool!
Jokin' about not holdin' my gold
Is my wife still cryin'? My food still cold?
D.S. Your wife? Yeah right, man, I hope she's a hot one
A.S. Why don't you tell me, since you told me I got one
D.S. Update me, baby, when spake me such a word?
A.S. Not half an hour since. Ya' heard?
D.S. I haven't see you since, since whence you sent me hence
With our pants and pence to the inn to pay our rents
So make some sense
A.S. Villain! Always imbecillin'!
You be illin'!

(**DJ STARTS BEATBOXING** a lá "*You be Illin*" by Run DMC)

A.S. The money, I gave it, and then you left
You returned, so soon, the cash bereft
You proceeded, to speak it, how I needed to come home
How some wife was waiting for me and my supper's getting cold

You be illin'!
D.S. I be illin'...
  The money you gave me...

  (The **DJ** *intentionally stops beatboxing.)*

D.S. *(to* **DJ***, pissed)* Yo?

  *(***DJ** *and* **ANTIPHOLUS** *congratulate each other.)*

D.S. I'm glad to see y'all actin' so silly
  But I don't know what you're talkin' about. What's the dilly?
A.S. What's the dilly?
D.S. Yeah, what the dilly is?
A.S. I'll show you what the dilly is

  (to the audience) I'ma show him what it really is

  (SNAP! **ANTIPHOLUS** *snaps* **DROMIO** *in the head yet again.)* **(BEAT #8 STARTS)**

A.S. I'm serious!
D.S. But I did what you said, Fred
  I delivered the bread, Fred
  Why you go ahead and smack me upside my head, Fred?
A.S. Cut your crappin' kid, I know what happened kid[14]
  You know as well as I do exactly what you did
  Because I joke around with you don't take it for granted
  See yours and my relationship...it's slanted!
  You be below and I be above
  Never let your sauciness jest upon my love
  If you make a common dish of my serious feast
  I'll be the landlord of victory and tear up your lease
  So unless you learn to jest with me at the proper time
  I guess you'll see
  My remedy – it's best to be my friend and not my enemy
D.S. Friend to the end brother, like no other
  "Enemy," you utter? But we're from the same mother!

　　　　So I guess you'll have it you treat me like doo-doo
　　　　Gettin' mad unnecessary snaps to my noodle
　　　　You're downright brutal, twisted like a strudel
　　　　Don't think you got me on a leash like a poodle
　　　　Your rap is some whack rap, I'm packin' my knapsack
　　　　Hat's off the hat-rack and I'll never be back, Jack
　　　　'Cause you walk the street and I walk the street and
　　　　Why oh why am I bein' beaten?
A.S. What you don't know?
D.S. 　　　　　　　　Nothin' but I'm beat down
A.S. Well then I'll tell you why I finally put my feet down
D.S. Wait, there's more, what's the wherefore?
　　　　For every why's got a wherefore, therefore
A.S. Why, first, for dissing me
　　　　And then wherefore, for urging it a second time
D.S. A...That doesn't rhyme. B...It has no reason
　　　　Why'm I being beaten, what's this, beat down season?
　　　　Well, thanks anyway
A.S. 　　　　　　　Why you thankin' me for something?
D.S. Because of that something you givin' me for nothin'
　　　　I was cuttin', struttin' shakin' floors, pushing buttons
　　　　Butterin' a muffin, when, then all of a sudden
A.S. Well let's face it you're faced with the pace that I'm makin'
　　　　I'm shakin' I'm bakin, disgracin' my placement? I'm chasin
D.S. A, stop it Bobbit, you rocket, a pocket, of Davey Crocket,
　　　　I don't mock it, allotted, I swear I got it, I got it
A.S. Man you hazy, you amaze me, you lazy baby, maybe
　　　　You shame me but you don't phase me, you crazy praise me
　　　　And I'm bastin' –
D.S. Basting?
A.S. 　　Basting!

D.S. Basting?

A/D. Ba-Ba-Ba-Ba-Ba-Basting!

A.S. The great game of rhyme has taught you to be funny
But son – Don't ever joke when you're talkin 'bout my money

D.S. I respect that, check that, in my memory bank
The only problem is – my memory's blank

A.S. You stinky weasel, all you do is smoke dust[15]
As we bounce from town to town, from dawn to dusk

D.S. From East

A.S. To West

D.S. No doubt

A.S. The best

D.S. Fully clothed

A.S. Undressed

D.S. Bottle rocket

A.S. *(bottle rocket noise)*

D.S. Stoopid fresh

A.S. The rest is history

D.S. Check the delivery

A.S. From pebbles

D.S. To boulders

A.S. From ankles

D.S. To shoulders

A.S. Trapper-keepers

D.S. To folders

A.S. Did you tell her?

D.S. I told her!

A.S. That we could go forever and the love will never stop

D.S. I'm the greatest lover in the world!

DJ. (**DJ** cuts the beat out and possibly scratches in or says something like, "Hold it right there!" or "Say what?" for example) **(BEAT #8 STOPS)**

(The following dialogue is spoken, not rapped:)

A.S. How are you the greatest lover in the world
   When you don't get no girls?
D.S. You don't know what I be gettin'
   I'm bettin' in a second all these ladies be sweatin'
A.S. Sweatin' 'cause they runnin', I know how you chase
   Panting like a dog with your tongue out your face
D.S. My tongue's out my face 'cause it's in another place[16]
A.S. Aw, man – you couldn't even steal first base
D.S. Who steals first base? Nobody steals first base.
   You can't steal first base.
A.S. Good point. But regardless, can you connect?
D.S. Just like that I step up to bat
   Take a practice swing before I do my thing
A.S. He said practice! That means he whack this![17]
D.S. No, master, I bait her with my hook
A.S. Well what if there ain't any fish left in the brook?
D.S. Elsewhere I look, you have to go where the fishes at
A.S. Oh yeah? Textbook, it's as simple as that
D.S. But there's nothing academic about it
   Try picking up a girl using logic? – I doubt it
A.S. Are you sayin' that females don't understand logic?
D.S. Not that they don't understand it, but they do unconsciously dodge it

   (**ADRIANA** *enters followed by* **LUCIANA**.)

A.S. Man, why you gotta stir up all this commotion?
D.S. Antipholus, turn around, two honeys approachin'
LUC. 1, 2 . . 3, 3, 8 – kick it sister!

   (**LUCIANA** *starts beatboxing and gets behind* **ADRIANA**,
   miming along with certain lines behind **ADRIANA** *while
   beatboxing.*)

ADR. Ay, ay, Antipholus, look strange and frown
   As if I am unknown to you in this town
   I am not valued, nor thy wife

Yet once I was, the love of your life
Once you vowed all flowers lost their smell
There was no magic, only evil spell
There was no calm, only violence
There was no song *(**LUCIANA** sings a high note)*, only [silence])
Basically the earth was completely dark
Unless it was lit up by my lovely spark
But how like a coin in a toilet I've been tossed out
But it's you that have spoiled it and you that has lost out
How quickly you would light up with anger
If I gave my body out to a stranger *(**LUCIANA** rubs down **ADRIANA**'s body.)*
You would spit at me and call me sow
Tear the skin from my whorish brow[18]
Cut from my hand the wedding ring
And break in two the sacred thing
But you have no right to accuse me
If you act like this I swear you're gonna lose me *(**LUCIANA** snaps and says "HA!")*
I am possessed by your adulterated sin
And through our bond I can feel it on my skin
If we are one and you are untrue
I digest the poison present in you *(**LUCIANA** mimes drinking poison and dying.)*
So please play fair and sleep in the proper bed
I live unstained and you…undishonored

LUC. HA!

A.S. Plead you to me fair dame? I know you not.
Call you me by name?

D.S.   – They both are hot

A.S. Word. Yo check it –
I just arrived in Ephesus *(**DROMIO** starts beatboxing.)*
This unknown pair of breastesses[19]

    Approaches me I guess this is
    The moment –
    To extend my hand
    And meet your sweet acquaintance ma'am
    Now do you understand we're brand new to this land?

LUC. – Hold it!
    Antipholus *(**ADRIANA** starts beatboxing.)*
    How can you act like this?
    She is your wife, your friend, my sister
    How can you so easily dismiss her?
    Even though women are a different gender
    And even though at home you are the largest member
    *(**ADRIANA**: "Uh-uh")*
    Remember, she sent Dromio to bring you to eat
    And he said that she said that he said that she said that
    she, he, she said, she uh…
    (Adriana's beatboxing trails off.) See, what happened was…
    Somebody saw someone somewhere???

ADR. In the street

LUC. In the street!

A.S. Dromio?

D.S. Me, yo?

ADR. You, YO!
    And this I know because you told me so *(**LUCIANA** beatboxes.)*
    You said he beat you up and claimed I'm not his wife
    Claimed my house as no part of his life

A.S. Did you converse, sir, with this gentle woman today?
    *(**DROMIO** beatboxes.)*
    What kinda trash out your ass did you gas and spray?[20]

D.S. Brother brother A., this girl, she's all about drama
    *(**ANTIPHOLUS** beatboxes)*
    First time I ever seen her in my life, scout's honor

A.S. But she just spoke everything you did speak *(**DROMIO** beatboxes.)*
    I'm at my peak, I'm ready to put you to sleep
    Cause you're a liar

D.S. Sire, I'm being blamed and framed *(**ANTIPHOLUS** beatboxes.)*

A.S. How can she thus then call us by our names? *(**DROMIO** beatboxes.)*

ADR. Why do you behave…like a knave? *(**LUCIANA** beatboxes, excitedly.)*
Pretending to be counterfeit with what you gave?
I met you in the mart now you're trying to thwart me
I'm starting to feel like you want to deport me
Husband, you seem to think from me you're exempt
But I hold you

ALL   Husband?

ADR.   in utter contempt
Come, I will fasten you to what's mine *(**LUCIANA** stops beatboxing.)*
Thou art an elm and I am the vine
I will play the weak wife and you the stronger state
But that only pushes me to communicate!

*(Between each "-ate" rhyme, **LUCIANA** makes record spinning noises.)*

Instigate! Emulate! Consummate! Masturbate![21]
Castrate! Dominate! Then close the gate!!
I will infect you like you infect me *(**LUCIANA**, **DROMIO**, and **ANTIPHOLUS** beatbox.)*
You can't reject me, we are bound in full effect the
Last thing I'll do is let you leave me
Let my intrusion clear your confusion do you believe me? *(Beatbox ends.)*
I need thee

*(All freeze except **ANTIPHOLUS**.)*

A.S. *(spoken)* To this wedlock theme she's sewed, it seems
Wha-what? Was I married to her in a dream?
Or do I dream now and just think I see all this?
What lies try to drive our ears and eyes amiss?
But until I get a clear grip on reality
I think I'll entertain this offered fallacy

D.S. He said
A.S. I think I'll entertain this offered fallacy
   (Break freeze.)
ADR. Dromio, do the justly deed, play the guard and wait
   If any little hussy comes rapping at the gate
   You tell them that your master dines above
   And although he's been errant he's now full of love
   Because his wife has forgiven his thousand idle pranks
   And for such a loving woman a man should give thanks
   Dromio, play the porter well
   *(**ADRIANA** exits.)*
A.S. Am I in Earth, in Heaven, or in Hell?
LUC. Earth
A.S. Am I asleep, awake, mad, or well-advised?
   I'm known unto them, but to myself disguised!
   This place is pretty freaky, I'm feelin sorta moody
   But this is an adventure. Besides, I might get booty
D.S. You get that, I'm going to play the porter.
LUC. Yes, very good, Dromio, and here's a quarter
   Come, come, Antipholus, let's not be fickle!
   *(**LUCIANA** and **ANTIPHOLUS OF SYRACUSE** exit.)*
D.S. Girl, this ain't nothing but a nickle
LUC. *(shutting door, exiting)* Suck my pickle!!
   (BEAT #9 STARTS)
D.S. Has my brother been hijacked in all this spontaneity?
   Now I'm trapped and trapped I hate to be
   Those chicken-heads are demons, schemin' on testament
   But you know what? I'm gonna make the best of it
   I'm overseein' a mansion, there's no time to brood
   And right now the place to be is this interlude
   Let me direct y'all's attention to the kid over there
   (points to DJ)

(**DJ** *scratches*) Oh, yeah
His cuts are so sweet , you gonna catch tooth decay
That's Our DJ – *(insert DJ Name)* – A K A
(insert DJ Nickname; ex: Bobheadz) so bob your heads
He's gonna make you freak and flinch with that 12-inch

(Music Break, DJ scratches for 8 bars.)

D.S. Take your middle finger and lick it
Now tear it up like an usher tears a theatre ticket
When I kick it, I kick it live, G
And when he scratches it's like he got poison ivy

(Music Break, DJ scratches for 8 bars.)

D.S. Feel free to shake your rump throughout the show
How you like us now? DJ, gimme one Moe, kid

(Music Break, DJ scratches for 8 bars – fades out.)
(BEAT #9 STOPS)

Damn, you tamed the track, made it look shrewish
Hold up, y'all. Someone's coming, and he looks mad Jewish

*(**DROMIO** exits.)*

Scene Four
Outside Antipholus of Ephesus' house

(**ANTIPHOLUS OF EPHESUS (A.E.)** *enters, followed by* **MC HENDELBERG (HEN)**. *MC Hendelberg wears a Run DMC-esque black fedora, glasses, with payes hanging off the glasses, and a big gold chain. The following dialogue is spoken.*)

A.E. Good MC Hendelberg, come in and sit down
'Tis not often I host the best jeweler in town

HEN. Hey, you're a good guy for the invite, I gladly will feast
Your wife's meatloaf beast is known west to east

A.E. Have you finished the big gold chain I commissioned
To make sweet my wife's sour disposition
If I'm late for dinner or I miss the hors-d'ouevres
Without flowers in hand to settle her nerves
Her affections dwindle, it's tough to rekindle
Pretty soon you'll start seeing my stuff come flying out the window

HEN. I'll bring the chain later by the light of the moon
The perfect time to make your wife swoon

A.E. Sounds like a plan my friend, you the man
Bring the chain later, I'll put the cash in your hand.

(**DROMIO OF EPHESUS** *enters.*)

A.E. Wassup Dromio, how you doing, herb?

D.E. Herb? Man, you've got some nerve
I've been scopin', seekin', your wife still be freakin'
Out, are you back on track or still tweakin'?

A.E. Tweakin'?

D.E. Yeah, your mind was crazy twisted.
Said your wife never existed, took my face, and double-fisted
Gave me a fat lip, knocked me to the Pharcyde of the curb
Remember that? Wassup Hendelberg?

HEN. Wassup
A.E. I'll hit you when I wanna, and if I'm gonna you just deal with it
Besides I haven't hit you in months
D.E.   Oh come real with it
You clowned me just today at the mart
A.E.   You're buggin'
D.E. You disowned your wife and home and me you started sluggin'
A.E. Alright, do you wanna get dropped?
D.E.   No, not again.
A.E. Or popped in the eye? 'Cause I am what I am
And that's an ill MC and I flow how I flow
I come and go as I please when I come and I go
Throughout Ephesus I'm known as a dependable
All rules are bendable, possessions lendable,
Debts extendable, all things I do commendable,
While you, you're expendable
'Cause you always blazin'[22]
Spendin' days and days smokin' haze, and it's amazing
You got Smokey Bear down on his knees,
Beggin' please 'cause you burn so many trees
Hit you I didn't, so zip it.
HEN.   You're donedidded
A.E. Good MC Hendelberg haven't you heard?
Say word.
HEN.   Vurd
A.E.   Dinner is served
HEN. If I'm under your roof I won't need a fiddle
But before I go in I've got this great riddle!
No one has solved it yet, together you must think:
For this is the riddle, the riddle of the sphinc:
A/D. The riddle of the sphinx?

HEN. No, the riddle of the sphinc
It's a part of the body but women have none
It's stiff to the touch and all men have one
It jumps when you cough, when you stretch it, it hardens
Eve put one in her mouth and got kicked out of the garden
It's surrounded by hair unless you choose to shave it
When licking the neck you might lubricate it
Men are from Mars, Women are from Venus
Some are longer than a stretched limousine is
I mean it's the cleanest, yours is the leanest
You don't have to be a genius, what is it? A –

D.E. – drive through in Sam Demas?

HEN. No, no that's not it

A.E. – How 'bout a drive through in Salinas?

HEN. No, it's not a drive through, you clots, I can't believe this

D.E. We need some more clues

A.E. I'm not sure if we've seen this

HEN. OK listen up, because I do mean this, I've said it in a variety of arenas,
It's the size a string bean is, strong like a wolverine is,
Cut in half with a guillotine this thing can make one fiendish or squeamish from teamsters to a seamstress,
Vick's vapor-rub will steam this, it brings some to their knees, like a queen, this Riddle, this isn't as hard as it seems this, I didn't dream this riddle, what is it?

A.E. I have no idea what you're talking about

HEN. It's an Adam's Apple! An ADAM'S APPLE, YOU SCHMUCKS!!!!
Alright, let's get this party started, right?

D.E. Right

HEN. Let's get this party started, quickly, alright?

A.E. Alright, enough of all this, let's go in and eat
The door seems to be locked, I'll give it a beat

(**ANTIPHOLUS** *knocks against gate as the beat starts.*)
(BEAT #10 STARTS)

A.E. Let us in, let us in, I pray thee let us in
Go kid, bid them kid to get us in

D.E. Bertha, Herbie, Lee Double Chin

HEN. Hello in there, is anyone listenin'

ALL. Let us in, let us in, I pray thee let us in

D.S. *(hidden/offstage)* Aye, when fowls have no feather and fish hath no fin

ALL. When fowls have no feather and fish hath no fin?

D.E. Uh…that wasn't Lee Double Chin
Hey, let us in, my master he stays in the street

D.S. *(hidden/offstage)* Let him stay in the street, gettin' blisters on his feet)

A.E. Did not I just hear what I thought I heard?

HEN. Say vurd

A.E. Vurd! This is absurd
It seems a new servant's bein' rude to me
Soupin' me, dupin' me, undertakin' mutiny
Who's inside my house that be actin' up?

(**DROMIO OF SYRACUSE** *emerges. The audience sees him but* **ANTIPHOLUS OF EPHESUS, DROMIO OF EPHESUS,** *and* **MC HENDELBERG** *do not. It remains this way for the rest of the scene.*)

D.S. Back it up, pack it in, but I have already begun
This is the House of Payne, so run or get done
It's the porter who was ordered to maintain headquarters
Keep at the borders, you trudgin' Muddy Waters
And I know your face is Redman

A.E. Oh, you are such a dead man

HEN. Who are you in there? Who let you in there?
Outside is the man who pays the bills round here

A.E. Yeah, show yourself louse, if you're a man not a mouse
You'd open that door and get the hell out my house[23]

D.E. Yeah, show yourself wussy, if you weren't a wussy
You'd come out that house, and we'd call you a wussy

D.S. Sticks and stones, may break my bones
You sherlocked outta your homes, Holmes

A.E. This is an outrage, dinner must begin
Let us in, let us in, I pray thee let us in

D.E. I'm here to check your gas, I'm with Con Edison[24]
Let us in, let us in, I pray thee let us in

HEN. Jehovah's Witness, we think you've sinned
Let us in, let us in, I pray thee let us in

D.S. What was that, I couldn't hear you, could you say it again?

ALL. Let us in, let us in, let us innnn…

D.S. I'm so rope, like a dope artichoke
Y'all can't cope, blowin' smoke, misanthrope

A.E. Alright, tell me your name? Why this must I endure?

D.S. I'm the porter, numb-nuts, you tell me yours!

A.E. Idiot coxcomb, this home I own, you know

D.S. Your home is bein' blown by the M to the C to the Dromio, oh-oh-io

D/D. Oh-io, oh-oh-io,
Oh-io, oh-oh-io,
Come on, everybody, do the baseball!

D.E. Oh, villain thou hast stolen both my song and my name
The one ne'er got me credit, the other gave me shame
If thou had been Dromio today in my place
You would have changed your name to Mr. Smacked-Up-Face

(**HENDELBERG** *begins false exit.*)

A.E. I'm gonna break down the door, MC Hendelberg, wait

D.S. Break any breaking here, and I'll break you knave's pate

A.E. Alright, this is offensive. You stop causin' drama

D.S. You wanna talk about offensive? Take a look at thy momma

ALL 3. Oooh....

D.S. Thy momma's so stupid

D.E.   Oh no he din't

D.S. It took her two hours to watch *60 Minutes*

D.E. Damn he just said took thy momma two hours to watch *60 Minutes*

A.E. You're a moron because my momma is your momma

D.E. Oh yeah?

A.E.   Yeah

D.E. Oh yeah... *(to* **D.S.**) Well, thy momma's so old...

D.S.   How old she's?

D.E. She don't wear Depends, she wear Definitelies

HEN. Thy momma's so Jewish...

> *(FREESTYLE for two minutes – this section is ad-libbed by the actor.* **HENDLEBERG** *is making this up as he goes and it doesn't and shouldn't make much narrative sense – when it becomes clear that it's a stream of consciousness the* **DJ** *should cut the beat out entirely – and* **HENDELBERG** *keeps going and going and somehow ends in a diss of some kind.)*

...smell that burn, wussy

(MUSIC STARTS)

A.E. You in there, let me speak to my wife

D.S. I'm speakin' with her and she says, "Get a life"

A.E. Get a life, well I've got something to say –

D.S. Oh, I'm sorry, bébé, but she just walked away
What was that? Oh, I'm coming, honey

A.E. Hey that's not funny

D.E.   That was funny

HEN.   That's freakin' funny

A.E. Let us in, let us in, I pray thee let us in

D.S. I'm busy with your wife makin' your next of kin

D.E./HEN. Ohhh!!!

A.E. Once I'm in, I'm gonna rip off your skin
    I'll give you a taste of your own medicine
    I'm going to tear you limb from limb from limb

ALL. Let us in, let us in, I pray thee let us in
    Let us in, let us in, tomatoes, let us in
    Let us in, let us in, I pray thee let us in
    (in song) I pray...thee...let...us.........innnnnnnnnn!
    (BEAT #10 STOPS)

(buzzer noise)

D.S. Thanks for playin', try again, you didn't win

D.E. Aw dang, we almost won

HEN. Have patience sirs, be grateful sirs
    I know this punk just said some hateful words
    But what's the worst thing about all this?
    No goodnight kiss? No meatloaf knish?
    We are all still healthy, there's no murder or injustice
    Relax yourself my good man, this advice please trust this
    Judge not before you know the true situation at hand
    That's just Common Sense; I can't do nothing for you man
    I'll send the chain by messenger, I've got to get home
    You win some, you lose some, see ya later, Shalom

(HENDELBERG *exits.)*

D.E. Master, you have been dishonored and scorned

A.E. My fear, Dromio, is that I have been horned
    Some other man sups and lies 'tween my sheets
    Rubbing her lips and kissing her feets
    Someone's commandeered my house and my treasure
    So we'll get our own booty at the house of pleasure
    There we'll find Desi, the most ferocious dame
    In all Ephesus there is none quite the same
    We will feast with her and thus shame my wife
    I'll show her, ha ha, you "Get a life!"

(Exuent all.)

*(**DJ** beatboxes and shows off some different beatbox skills – approximately one minute.)*

Scene Five
Inside Antipholus of Ephesus' house

(**ANTIPHOLUS OF SYRACUSE, ADRIANA,** *and* **LUCIANA** *enter. All three carry plates. Antipholus' plate still has food on it.*)

LUC. That was a wonderful meatloaf dinner, sister

ADR. Thank you, sister

A.S. Is that all you got is meatloaf?

ADR. Well you never had a problem with it before

A.S. I never ate here before!

(**ADRIANA** *grabs the dishes and starts to exit.*)

ADR. Wait 'til you see what's for dessert

(**ADRIANA** *mouths "Asshole" and exits.*)

LUC. (BEAT #11 STARTS) Alright, Antipholus, you just listen up mister
What kind of game are you playing with my sister?
She loves you, she loves you, you have no equal
She loves you, yeah, yeah, like the Beatles
Or the bugs and the birds so don't make her blue
If birds and bees do it, so should you two
If you're feeling someone else in the sack
Come clean with the facts cause that is wiggity-whack
I am down with truth and down with honesty
But best believe I'm not down with O.P.P.
I know what it stands for, I'll say it with malice
O.P.P. – 'Othello's Pleasure Palace'
A brothel next to St. Betty's Cathedral
Where for a few evil g's they please'll your weasel[25]
Which I know you frequent on occasion
And meet with a girl with whom you have relations
Don't think I don't know what you do after dark
I may be stupid, but I'm not smart
You're breaking my sister's heart, you creep
Now go to her and say something sweet

(**ANTIPHOLUS** *says nothing, lost in her eyes.*)

LUC. – – Something sweet!

A.S. Sweet mistress, can I kiss this?
Your hand? Make me understand
See, you exude mad knowledge and grace
And truth radiates from your face
I can see that you're an honest case
So teach me dear creature, how to think and speak
'Cause I'm feeble, I'm full of errors, I'm shallow and I'm weak
But your smirk and your quirks change the blood in my veins
Before I go further, girl, what's your name?

LUC. Luciana

A.S. Luciana?

LUC. Yeah, Luciana, hello?

A.S. Luciana, check it
Lu, can I make sweet love to you?[26]
Can you change my sky from grey to blue?
We can catch a flick, eat some Japanese food
Maybe you could wear something I could see thru
Say Lu-ciana
Lu-ciana
Lu-ciana
Lu-ciana
Your voice sends chills down the back of my spine
And I love the way your wide eyes peer into mine
Let's face it, you're a hotty with a dope ass body[27]
Can you and I get sweaty like the guy who knows karate
Or maybe ju-jitsu, whatever glove fits you
I like the way your body moves and girl I can't resist you
It's true, it's you, I've finally found you
The girl of my dreams and I wanna be around- –
Lu-ciana
Lu-ciana…

LUC. I like that part

A.S. Lu-ciana
Lu-ciana

*(Two **BACK-UP SINGERS** enter and dance and sing along with **ANTIPHOLUS**.)*

BACK. Lu, can I make sweet love to you
Can you change my sky from gray to blue
Lu, can I make sweet love to you
Change my sky from gray to blue

A.S. Lu-ciana *(with **BACK-UP SINGERS**)*
Lu-ciana
Lu-ciana
Lu-ciana

*(**BACK-UP SINGERS** exit.)*

A.S. I promise you Lu, I can be trusted
Your sisters' not my wife, and her face is all busted
She's tore up from the floor up, her breath smells like tuna
But you're more up from the floor up than the moon, I mean, the luna
Serenade ya in Spanish, woo you in Swahili
Ask you in German, "Was ist die dilly?"
Say that's cool in Portuguese like "Esto es coolo"
Curse your sister in Italian "Va fangulo"
Tag your name on stalls while I'm sittin in the loo
I'll say something in French like *(French accent)* "I love you"
But the language we both know is the language of love
And regardless of the tongue, you'll always fly above
Labels, words, copies, imitations
I wanna be a citizen of Luciana Nation

*(**BACK-UP SINGERS** enter and dance and sing with **ANTIPHOLUS** and **LUCIANA**.)*

BACK. Lu, can I make sweet love to you
Can you change my sky from gray to blue
Lu, can I make sweet love to you
Change my sky from gray to blue

A.S. Lu-ciana
Lu-ciana
Lu-ciana
Lu-ciana

(**LUCIANA** *is caught up in the song.*)

LUC. Lu-ciana
Lu-ciana
Lu-ciana
Lu-ciana

(**ANTIPHOLUS OF SYRACUSE** *goes to DJ booth and talks into microphone.*)

A.S. *(from DJ Booth, in deep baritone)* Lu – Luciana?

(**LUCIANA** *crosses herself, confused.*)

A.S. *(spoken)* No, I'm not God. I'm up over here behind you. I know that I only met you 20 minutes ago girl and I know my voice just dropped like three octaves, but I want to spend the rest of my life with you girl. Lu girl, it's all about you. Keep shakin' that thing.

(**LUCIANA** *spins in ecstasy, almost falling off the stage as everyone continues singing.*)

ALL. Lu-ciana
Lu-ciana
Lu-ciana
Lu-ciana

(**LUCIANA** *stops herself, snapping out of the fantasy.*)
(BEAT #11 STOPS)

LUC. Stop! Stop! *(to* **BACK-UP SINGERS** *and* **DJ***)* Who are you people? – you don't live here.

(**LUCIANA** *pushes* **BACK-UP SINGERS** *offstage.*)

LUC. *(to* **ANTIPHOLUS***)* What are you mad that you reason so?

A.S. Not mad, try glad. But mad? Hell, no[28]

LUC. I see the lust behind your eye

A.S. Lust and love are together tied

LUC. Gaze where you should or you will lose your sight

A.S. On you, sweetness, all day and all night

LUC. Don't call me "sweet," call my sister so

A.S. Your sister's sister

LUC. That's my sister

A.S. No, it's you

> (**LUCIANA** *tries to do the math in her head and then figures it out.*)

LUC. *(in a man's voice)* Oh, right
(back to woman's voice) Oh…whoops

A.S. It is yourself, my own self's better part
My eye's clearer eye, my hearts dearer heart
My food, my fortune, my sweet hope's aim
My whole earth's heaven and my heaven's claim
Because now I see heaven, and you're my set of stairs
God bless these beautiful locks of golden hair

LUC. Say this to my sister

A.S. Her hair is red

LUC. What scene is this?

A.S. Did you hear what I said?
You're the one I want, you're the one I need
Without requisition this soul's bound to bleed
So put your hand in mine and we can follow the stars
We'll skip town tonight and make the universe ours

LUC. Oh my god, man, you need to sit still
I'm going to go find my sister and take a few chill pills

> (**LUCIANA** *exits.*)

DJ. *(singing)* Lu-ciana, Lu-ciana, Lu-ciana, Lu–

A.S. Yo – would you cut it out?

DJ. I can't help it, yo' – it's mad catchy…

    (**DROMIO OF SYRACUSE** *enters.*)

A.S. How now Dromio where runn'st thou so fast from?

D.S. Do you know me? Am I Dromey the phony emcee assasin?

A.S. I know you why you askin'? A phony emcee passin'?

D.S. Like you, I gotta wife too

A.S.   Who, what happened?

    (**BEAT #12 STARTS**)

D.S. I was in the house, the porter, in full effect
    When I caught a whiff of something sweet and decided to check
    Where it was comin' from, I wound up in the kitchen
    I was on a mission

A.S.   Everybody listen

D.S. There was meatloaf on the counter, meatloaf on the stove
    Meatloaf a la meatloaf a la meatloaf a la mode
    Sweet potato pie with marshmallow toppin'
    Lobster bisque, that and this, so I started ploppin'
    Scoops on a dish, I sat down to chow
    When all of a sudden…BLAOW!
    The door swung open, my fork went flyin'
    There stood the biggest girl in the world

DJ.   Stop lyin'

D.S. On the spherical tip spread like Miracle Whip
    Same length head to toe as she was hip to hip
    She scooped me like a corn chip scooping…
    Dip Dip, dive in her grip, I arrived
    Pound for pound, ounce for ounce, frame by frame
    She drew me to her face and with bass said her name
    "Bertha – I'm as big as the eartha
    The hip in hip hop from top to turfa

D.S. Push me off a cruise ship, you've got waves to surf-a
Push me down a decline, you got mad inertia
Fee Fie Foe Fum"
You think the story's over but it's only just begun
Somebody, anybody, everybody scream

A.S. Aghhhhhhhhhhhhh!!!!

She said, "Dromio what you doin' in the kitchen all alone
You know all morning I've been waitin' by the phone
I thought we had a date to go walkin' in the park
Now I'm gonna spank you on your fish shaped beauty mark"
I said, "Hark! Hold up! Wait a minute! Time out!
How do you know my name and all about my brook trout
Birthmark that's on my butt – that's my biz
What are you a witch? What kinda town this is?"
She said, "You're my husband and I love thee so
Up up up and away we go."
I thought, "I'm doomed," over her head so high
Excuse me while I kiss the sky **(MUSIC STOPS)**

(DROMIO and ANTIPHOLUS play air guitar and make noises like the guitar lick in "Purple Haze")

D/A. Derrr-nerrrr-nerrr-nerrr-nerrr-nerr-nerr-nerr-nerr

D.S. Just like that I'm on her **(MUSIC STARTS)** back, going up, up, up, up
And Bertha's going blub, blub, blub, blub, blub, blub
I had no headroom, you can ask the ceilin'
Heading for the bedroom and I got this funny feelin'

A.S. Fee to the fie to the fo to the fum

D.S. She didn't want me to go because she wanted to –
Come on y'all[29]
Somebody anybody everybody scream

D/A. Aghhhhhhhhhhhhhhh!!!!

D.S. Ok, now it's on
Bertha had me in her room, and in her palm
She was so damn B – I – G
A.S. Notoriously!
D.S. She drew me
Inches from her large mouth
Now I'm getting treated like a bass ale stout, suckin' on me[30]
With tons of pressure, heat and wetness
A big fat passionate, big fat wet kiss
I know it's hard to digest this
But, party people, I'm gonna confess this
I was drippin', she was trippin', my clothes she started strippin'
Smothering my bozack and bitin' on my lip then[31]
She started strippin', revealing all her blubbery
A.S. Her bra size?
D.S. 144 triple double Z
A.S. Damn!
D.S. With any other girl this situation would be killer
But see, she looked like Godzilla
I screamed in terror, she thought it was elation
She bear-hugged me, cut off my circulation
And I blacked out (**MUSIC STOPS**)

(Lights blackout.)

A.S. Yo, this is wacked out
BOTH. Fee fie foe fum
Fee fie foe fum (**MUSIC STARTS**)
Fee fie foe fum
Let's do this one more time and then the song is done
Somebody, anybody, everybody scream
D/A. Aghhhhhhhhhhhhhhh! (**BEAT #12 STOPS**)

(Lights come up. **DROMIO** *is in* **ANTIPHOLUS**' *arms.)*

D.S. When I awoke, I awoke with a jolt and she was gone

A.S. Dromio –

D.S. Yeah?

A.S. – get the hell out of my arms[32]
Dromio, I must confess we are possessed
This town's got the better of us

D.S. Plus the best

A.S. Now your ass is wrapped up in a big fat mess[33]
With some big fat lass in some big fat dress
With some big fat breasts who wants big fat sex
I'm saying dig that text

D.S. I need to rid that stress!

A.S. I'm getting mad vexed

D.S. Well, I'm getting mad scared

A.S. I'm sayin, let's be out, just make sure we're prepared
Get back to the hotel, get our things together
Reserve us a jet and pray for good weather

D.S. Like a man who runs from a gun for his life
I will fly from Big Bertha who says she's my wife

*(**DROMIO OF SYRACUSE** exits.)*

A.S. Oh, man, something' funny goin' on in this place and we're in it
Things are gettin weirder in this city by the minute

*(**BOBBY (BOB)** the Bike Messenger enters, messenger bag slung over his shoulder, carrying a large gift-wrapped box.)*

BOB. MC Antipholus!

A.S. How'd you know my name?

BOB. *(struggling with the rhythm)* I've been lookin' for you, I've got a package
Here you go, there's a letter on it
I've been riding all over and this thing is hefty
Thank, God, I found you this is my last drop off!
I love to rap, man, I wish I could rock
Never mind, could I just get your sig –

A.S. My John Hancock?
BOB. Whoa…you're really good
A.S. It's easy to rhyme, now just tell me where I sign…
BOB. Just sign on the dotted… just sign by the X
A.S. If you're feelin uptight, it's alright, just let go
   If you get an ounce of pounce in your bounce, you'll get yo'
   Rhythm intact and you'll be spittin them raps
   Your friends be givin you daps while you be rippin' them tracks
BOB. Whooooaaaaaaa!
A.S. Practice makes perfect, soon you'll be rappin
BOB. Alright dude, I'll try, who knows what'll happen

   (**BOBBY** *starts to exit then realizes –*)

BOB. Whooooaaaaaaa!!!!!
A.S. Drop me something

   (**BOBBY** *drops clipboard.* **ANTIPHOLUS** *retrieves and hands it back to him.*)

A.S. No, man. A verse. I'll beat box for you

   (**ANTIPHOLUS** *beatboxes while* **BOBBY** *attempts a rhyme.*)

BOB. My name is Bobby, I get on my bike
   I drive around town and I do what I want to do
A.S. Yeah, you killed it, man!
BOB. Yeah, see you later, crocodile!

   (**BOBBY** *exits.*)

A.S. This is a heavy package and it's addressed to me
   The return address says Hendelberg's family jewelery
   (*reading in Hendelberg's voice*) "MC Antipholus, here's the chain you ordered
   If you're reading this note it means that you got it
   Here's the receipt, subtotaling one G
   You can pay me later tonight at O.P.P.

P.S. Did I ever tell you the riddle of the Sphinc?"

(aside to audience, normal voice) I think he means the riddle of the sphinx

(Hendelberg's voice) "No. I mean the riddle of the sphinc! Never mind that

I just ran out of room on this piece of pap-"

(normal voice) See what I'm sayin? This town is mad whack

I gotta get the hell out of here before that guy comes back[34]

(**ANTIPHOLUS** *starts to exit then returns and opens box, pulls out an enormous Chain and puts it on.*)

A.S. *(to audience)* Wha-what? Wha-what?
I don't know anyone who'd be so vain
To refuse the offer of such a nice chain

(**ANTIPHOLUS** *exits.*)

Scene Six
The Mart

(**ANTIPHOLUS OF EPHESUS** *and* **DROMIO OF EPHESUS** *enter.*)

(BEAT #13 STARTS)

A.E. That no good, good-for-nothing, skanky slut (**D.E.** "*Slut!*")[35]

Who calls herself my wife – I'll kick her funky butt (**D.E.** "*Butt!*")

'Cause I'm still in a rut (**D.E.** "*Rut!*"), locked and stuck out

And when I meet that servant he'll get knocked the (**D.E.** "*Beep*") out

Here's the plan, my man, are you on it?

D.E. Yeah I'm on it!

A.E. Take a trip down to Ephesus Electronic

Get a mic and a cord, and a fat ass amp[36]

You got it?

D.E. Mic and a cord and an amp –

A.E. You da champ! (**D.E.** "*Champ!*")

We'll set it up outside my house and turn it up to red (**D.E.** "*Red!*")

Then I'll sing my damn lungs out till the speakers are dead (**D.E.** *Dead!*)

I'll sing the extended 15 minute version of – **(MUSIC STOPS)**

(singing) "I would do anything thing for love"

BOTH. *(singing)* "But, I won't do that. No, I won't do that"

A.E. I'll just **(MUSIC STARTS)** rant and rave, holler and curse (**D.E.** "*Curse!*")

And when they think it gets bad it'll just get worse (**D.E.** "*Worse!*")

They'll open the gates and surrender I intend ta

Put my wife in a blenda, and her frienda, change his genda

Call him Brenda, Nah– I'm sayin'?

D.E. You said it

A.E. Now go get it

D.E. Aight, bet, kid –

A.E. Revenge is hungry and it's time I fed it
I spot MC H comin' round the curb
Hurry up, Dro, now get a move on,

D.E. Vurd!
I'll be back in a bit like lickety-split
So we can figure out how all this trickery hit
Dickery-dock, take a look at the rickety clock…tower
I'll be back in less than half an hour **(MUSIC STOPS)**

*(***DROMIO OF EPHESUS*** exits.* **MC HENDELBERG** *enters. Spoken.)*

HEN. MC Antipholus – I'm sorry I couldn't make it, I got caught by the misses
She had tickets to a documentary about Gefilte fishes
It was pretty good but in Yiddish without translation
Never mind that-ish, here's my situation
I need the money for the chain, 'cause I got a debt across the river
And if I don't pay right away, I'll end up chopped liver

A.E. I wish I could help you but my pockets are empty
Why don't you bring the chain to my wife and tell her I sent thee
She'll fork over the ducats when she sees that necklace
So you can get your money and you'll become debtless

HEN. So you'll bring the chain to her, am I right?

A.E. Not if you're in a rush and need money tonight
It makes more sense for you to take her the locket

HEN. Well, sir, I will, is it in your pocket?

A.E. It's not with me, it's with he who made it

HEN. Just hand it over turkey my humor has faded
I know you've got it

A.E. I never saw it

HEN. I had it delivered!

A.E. Oh, cry me a river!

HEN. Now give the chain back!

A.E. You sent me jack!

HEN. I have proof **(MUSIC STARTS)** here's the slip that you signed for my package
Now hand over the chain or hand over my cabbage

A.E. I never signed any slip, any paper, or receipt
How can you stand there and lie through your teeth?

HEN. I made it, then I gave it,
Now you fake you didn't take it?

A.E. You're crooked!

HEN. How can I take it if you took it?!

A.E. I never saw a trace of the chain in the first place

HEN. You're a disgrace

A.E. You debase me to my face?

*(**ANTIPHOLUS** begins to walk away.)*

HEN. Don't walk away mister

A.E. You're a sheister

HEN. Now I'm in the middle of a jewelry heist, er...
It's a hold up

A.E. Go fold up shop

HEN. I'll call a cop

A.E. Go call a cop

HEN. I'll call two cops!

A.E. And I still won't stop

HEN. Police...!

A.E. Money please, let them send ten cars and all of their back-up
Then sit back and watch them belly laugh and crack up
At this dude selling jewelry who's really peddling foolery
They'll laugh so hard they'll laugh you back to Hebrew schoolery

HEN. It's all the same with you young rappers and rhymers
Your generation's got no respect for old-timers

I lived through the Sixties, I'd love to go back
I passed around the peace pipe but I never smoked crack[37]
I know the vocab, "My baby's got back"
And you're never too old to know when somebody's whack

(**COP** *enters from back of audience. He has his own odd rhythm and personality.*)

COP. Alright, let the beat stop!! **(BEAT #13 STOPS)**
I'm the cop
I was sitting over at the donut shop
Heard my name dropped
Came over to find out the root of the ruckus

(**COP** *walks onstage.*)

HEN. Well sir, Mr. Mashuganna here tried to kick me in the tuchus
All the hours I devoted

A.E. So you claim

HEN. Expenses I unloaded

A.E. For the supposed chain

HEN. Boy did I get bloated

A.E. I swear I'm bein' framed

HEN. Just to make him a special shmutzka[38]

A.E. Which I never saw in my life

HEN. To hang around the neck of some hooker

A.E. You're not talking about my wife

HEN. Oh the chutzpah!

Oy vey, what a low blow	**A.E.** That's a low blow,
That he won't pay what he knows he owes	you might as well go Or we will stay not friends but foes

COP. Hold your horses…and I do like horses
(*into his collar*) This is Pawn 7 to the Rook
(*back to* **A.E.**) I need the name of the crook

Did anybody get shot?
Do you know how to do the robot?
Is this a first time offense or have you been caught
Before? You can't ignore the details
Is this about females?
I need to know who slept with who and when
Was his name Ira or was his name Sven?
What were they like under the covers?
Can I get your phone number?
You have the right to remain silent but I wouldn't recommend it
I have to tell you that 'cause it's an amendment

A.E. I will not remain silent, I have been accused and threatened
Of stealing this man's chain and being in debt and
I have no criminal record take a look at my file
If you want my opinion this quack is senile

(**COP** *draws his gun and points it at* **ANTIPHOLUS**.)

COP. Alright, listen up you sniveling punk
Something stinks and I'm here to find out who stunk
Put your dirty hands in the sky unless you wanna die
Ephesus is a clean town and I'll tell you why
'Cause crooks like you don't get a chance to do the dirty
"Little girlies are free as birdies and they never get hurty"
'Cause the laws are sturdy like a rock
The bad guys come clean and they never walk
You hear that distant clink? That's a link
A chain link on a prison fence slammin'
From now on it's 'Yes sir' and 'Thank you Mammen'
Mammen's the warden, he's a tough Irish brute
He's stiff when you're good and even stiffer when you're cute[39]
So start reading up on your Gaelic and collecting four leaf clover
Or expect more than Irish Spring when you bend over

(DROMIO OF SYRACUSE enters.) **(BEAT #14 STARTS)**

D.S. Master there's a flight to Epidamnum and I know that place is random
But at 10 o'clock we leavin' and at midnight we'll be landin'
In a high fly slammin' big, rigged Concord
All our supplies I've stored aboard
I've got our fraughtage, our freightage, that means our cargo
An aromatic resin balsabum balm bargo
Alcohol, spirits, lemons, limes
For us to get stupid then rock doo doo rhymes

COP. Slow down, sonny *(to* **DJ***)* You too, sonny. Slow down, yeah, slow down *(***DJ*** slows down the track.)* Alright why don't you just stop it altogether *(***DJ*** stops the track.)* **(BEAT #14 STOPS)**
(to **D.S.***)* You come in bouncin' like a bunny
You're gonna get skinned like a wabbit
I'm a trigger happy hunter so dagnabbit
Put your hands in the air and elab it!

D.S. Elabbit?

COP. Elaborate, hello, your situation

D.S. My brother sent me to get plane reservations

HEN. See he's tryin' to stiff me, he's gonna skip town
Don't think I don't know you, you don't think I'm down?

D.S. Who's this Jewish guy and what drugs has he been on
And screw this cop and the horse he rode in on

COP. Oh look at me, aren't I funny, I'm a real rapscallion
I'll blow off your nads if you rag on my stallion[40]
She's an I-talian thoroughbred
So why don't you take that sorry little butt of yours

back home to bed
Her name's Bessie, craps in a bucket, never messy

*(As **COP** thinks of Bessie, he unconsciously begins massaging **DROMIO**'s chest. **COP** becomes aware of what he's doing.)*

Alright, that never happened, never!
We got your man, Turkeyburger –

HEN. – Hendelberg

COP. Whatever

*(**ANTIPHOLUS OF EPHESUS** hands **DROMIO OF SYRACUSE** a big key from his pants pocket. **COP** ties up **ANTIPHOLUS**' hands with a rope and starts to lead him offstage, tugging on the rope.)*

A.E. To Adriana go give her this key
Tell her in the desk covered with meatloaf tapestry
Is a purse of ducats which she must send
My arrest in the streets, the money will mend
Take heed, with speed, I must be freed, succeed

D.S. Indeed, it's agreed, I'ma get you what you need
I shall

A.E. Proceed…

*(**DROMIO**, **ANTIPHOLUS**, and the **COP** exit.)*

HEN. And continue to rock the mic
Well I'm M.C. Hendelberg the head of my crew
I dance around town as I kick up my shoes
I like mu-zik and I play mine loud
Shalomies to my homies, time to make moms proud

*(Offstage actors sing Hava Nagila as **HENDELBERG** does a Jewish breakdance for a few bars. He ends with a triumphant:)*

HEN. Hey!!

*(**HENDELBERG** exits.)*

Scene Seven
Inside Antipholus of Ephesus' house

(ADRIANA and LUCIANA enter.)

(BEAT #15 STARTS)

ADR. So you're saying that my husband tried to get you into bed?

LUC. Yes, Adriana, that's what I just said

ADR. Are you sure you didn't just mishear?

LUC. No…he made it pretty clear
First he praised my beauty, then my speech

ADR. What? –

LUC.   – Have patience, I beseech

ADR. He praised your speech, what the hell did he say?[41]

LUC. Well, like, like, like, okay
First, he said he knew some guy who knew karate
And then he said he, like, liked my body
He said he knew Swahili and that he was, like, really
Into me and sang this song, it was so silly:
Loo-chee-something, loo-chee-something
Loo-chee-something, something something
Loo –

ADR.   – ciana?

LUC. Not now, sister, I'm trying to remember the words to the song…

(DROMIO OF SYRACUSE *enters. He hands the key to* **ADRIANA.)**

D.S. Here go, the desk, the purse, no time to ask

LUC. How hast thou lost thy breath?

D.S.   By running fast

ADR. Where is my damn husband, I prithee tell

D.S. He's in a place that's worse, that's worse than hell
A blue –

L/A.   Who?

D.S. — devil in a bomber got him
I'm surprised —
L/A. — why?
D.S. — guy mighta already shot him
He was hard as steel
LUC. Steel?
D.S. I'm talkin' tough
ADR. Tough?
D.S. A fiend
LUC. Whatcha mean?
D.S. Pitiless and rough
ADR. Rough?
D.S. A wolf
LUC. Really?
D.S. A willy all in buff
ADR. Buff?
D.S. Armed with the badge, gun, hat, and handcuffs
ADR. Enough, what's the matter?
D.S. It's bad and getting badder
ADR. Arrested?
D.S. You guessed it
ADR. Police?
LUC. Thank you
D.S. You're welcome
ADR. *(giving key to **D.S.**)* Go help him!
D.S. *(holding out key to **LUC.**)* The G's!
LUC. The who?
D.S. Money
LUC. Honey
ADR. Lemon
D.S. Lime
LUC. Pony
ADR. Dromi
D.S. O — me

LUC.		Oh my!

ADR. What are we

D.S.		Doing?
LUC.		Funny word game!
ADR.	We have to	
D.S.	Stop this	
LUC.	Gold chain	
	Pony	
ADR.	{Elephant}	{ }=ad-libbed
D.S.		{Donkey}
LUC.	Pony	
ADR.	{Rhinoceros}	
D.S.		{Spider}
LUC.	Pony	
ADR. *(relenting)*	Pony	
D.S.		{Ostrich}
LUC.	Pony	
ADR.	Pony	
D.S.	{Orangutang}	
LUC. *(screams at **D.S.**)*		PONY! **(MUSIC STOPS)**

D.S. Pony!!!

LUC. Yay, we all said pony

ADR. Just tell me what happened 'cause I ain't havin' it

D.S. I don't remember what happened, I was too busy elabbin' it

L/A. Elabbin it?

D.S.	Elaborate, hello?	
LUC.		Hi

D.S. (MUSIC STARTS) Never mind elabbin' it, fetch money from the cabinet

ADR.	Go fetch it, sister.	
LUC.	Which key is it?	
D.S./ADR.		The one with the tag on it!

(LUCIANA throws a bag of money to DROMIO.)

LUC. Here's the money that you asked for, Dro
D.S. Having so much dough, I'm good to go, so …

(DROMIO OF SYRACUSE exits.)

ADR. My life is ruined, my life is over
    Not only is my husband a Casanova
    But now he's a thief and our honor's discarded
    My sister's dumb
LUC.   Huh?
ADR.   No, she's retarded
    Everything that could go wrong has gone wrong
    It just can't get any worse I just can't go on
    Would I were a widow and no weeping willow
    Time to go to my room and cry in my pillow
(BEAT #15 FADES & STOPS)

(ADRIANA exits.)

LUC. Oh, my poor sister, he's broken her heart
    And it's all my fault, I wish I were smart
    If only there were some way that we could all win
    Like if, instead of liking me, like, Antipholus had a twin
    And, like, he liked me, and, like, I liked him
    And we got married and had a girl named Gwendolyn
    And had a white picket fence around our small house
    And we bought her a pony and a dollhouse

(LUCIANA laughs crazily, caught in the fantasy. Then her head hurts.)

LUC. Ow, I think I broke something.
    Wait, this is important, I need a plan
    I must turn things back to normal if I can
    Now who could help me solve this in a cinch
    Wait, I know: Dr. Pinch! Dr. Pinch!

(LUCIANA exits.)

Scene Eight
The Mart

(**ANTIPHOLUS OF SYRACUSE** *enters, wearing the big Chain. Offstage voices are heard making commotion.*)
(BEAT #16 STARTS)

A.S. Everywhere I go, people givin' me skin
　　They sayin' "Whassup?" and they callin' me friend
　　Strangers in the street, they look me in the eye
　　They callin' out my name, they catchin' me by surprise
　　I love when someone looks at you as if they know you
　　Shakes your hand and then passes you the spliff they rolled you[42]
　　Stuffin' money in your pockets that they owed you
　　And when you ask them why they said "I told you"
　　No explanations necessary feelin' like the king
　　Landed in a brand new town that's got swing
　　People like

(**C-FAKE (C-FAK)** *and* **RECEIVE CAT (R CAT)** *enter. They both wear flannel shirts and beanie/skull caps – a la Cypress Hill.* **RECEIVE CAT***'s hat is pulled over his eyes. Thus, he cannot see.*)

C-FAK.　　　　　　Antipholus
R CAT.　　　　　　　　　　How you do?
A.S. I'm like, "Fine, even though I don't know you."
C-FAK. Yo, yo Antipholus…Get this
　　It's another phat shipment that you can't miss
R CAT.　　　　　　　　　　You can't miss!
C-FAK. My favorite musical's the *Pirates of Penzance*
　　We like to roll through Ephesus doin' our dance
R CAT.　　　　　　　　We do a dance!
C-FAK. (*passing cigar to* **A.S.***)* Here's the weed and the trees you need[43]
　　We'll catch you later at the O.
R CAT.　　　　　　　　　　　　P.P.!

C-FAK. Bomb-itty, bye, bye
La, la, la, la, la, la, la, la

(**C-FAKE** *and* **RECEIVE CAT** *exit* – **RECEIVE CAT** *slams into the set as he leaves.*)

A.S. Everywhere I go, people givin' me skin
They sayin' "Whassup?" and they callin' me friend
Strangers in the street, they look me in the eye
They callin' out my name, they catchin' me by –

(**DROMIO OF SYRACUSE** *enters.*)

D.S. Surprise!
Yo Antipholo, check it out I got the dough

(**DROMIO** *hands* **ANTIPHOLUS** *the bag of gold.*)

A.S. Yo, Dromio, I didn't ask for no—Whoa!
Did you talk to a pilot? Did you get a plane?

D.S. Pilot? Plane? Are you insane in the brain?
Act like you know – that's some stuff I already got for you

A.S. Turn around brother man 'cause you still got a lot to do!
Phone the operator, ask 'em for an airline
So we can catch a flight tonight, aight?

D.S. Fine!
I'm beginnin' to feel like there's just no end
I mean I do things once and then I do 'em again
I'm beginnin' to feel like there's just no end
I mean I do things once and then I do 'em again
I'm beginnin' to feel like there's just no end
I mean I do things …

A.S. Dromio, get the hell outta here![44]

(**DROMIO** *exits. A transvestite prostitute,* **FELICIO** (**FEL**), *pops his body around the corner, revealing his bare midriff.*)

FEL. Are you lookin for love?

A.S. Hell no! (**FELICIO** *exits.*) But I found it[45]

Or it found me and now I feel grounded
'Cause I don't' wanna leave 'til I find Luciana
I wanna be her papi and she could be my mama
I never much believed in that love at first sight
Never thought I could fall for a girl in one night
All it took was a look, exchanged between our eyes
And suddenly I'm lifted, without even getting high[46]
Everywhere I go, people givin' me skin
They sayin' *(Offstage:* **ALL** *"Whassup?")* and they callin' me *(***ALL.** *"friend!")*
Strangers in the street, they look me in the eye
They callin' out my name, they catchin' me by surprise
They be callin' out my name, catchin' –

DESI. *(Offstage)* Antipholus! (**BEAT #16 FADES**)

(**BEAT #17 STARTS**) *(*DESI *enters. She stops music with gesture.)* (**MUSIC STOPS**)

DESI. Is that it? Is that the chain you promised me?

A.S. I didn't promise you this chain ma'am, honestly

DESI. What did I tell you 'bout callin' me ma'am!

A.S. Oh I'm sorry miss, I just don't understand –

DESI. Miss? Kiss my ass sugar[47]
Save that sweet-talkin' for some other fly hooka
Desi ain't no pigeon-stool
You can't get up early enough to pull the wool
Hand it over on the double

A.S. Now, look sweetie, I don't want any trouble

DESI. Well, you got all the trouble, slimfast
Give it up or I'm gonna bitchslap your bona fide ass[48]

A.S. You muggin' me?

DESI. This ain't about a robbery, child
This about that sweet-ass chain you promised me child[49]
If I was muggin' you
I'd already be done with you
Don't play dumb with me
You had dinner in my company
You ain't stumpin' me

If I was bass, you'd be bumpin'me
But I'm not base, baby, I'm royalty, all about loyalty
Don't go back on your word that's gonna piss Desi off royally
And competitors are metaphors for a set of whores[50]
Getting' expeditiously cooked by my lyrical
The chain...

*(**ANTIPHOLUS** hands over the Chain. **DESI** purrs. **ANTIPHOLUS** barks, curiously. **DESI** purrs again. **ANTIPHOLUS** barks back, this time less timidly. Exchange continues until **DESI** screams and sends **ANTIPHOLUS** running offstage. **DESI** signals music to start and puts on the chain.)* **(MUSIC STARTS)**

DESI. *(cont.)* How's it look girls?
Well you just saw the madam's magic
Tell me I'm not charismatic
If I come with static that's the breaks
What Madam Desi wants, Madam Desi takes
Today during dinner on the couch
I caught his ass looking down my blouse[51]
He was talkin' bout his trick ass spouse
And hows she locked him out of his own house
What type of woman treats her man like that
If that was me, I'd knock a door down flat
But he's a puss like that and I told him so
"Get yourself a roughneck ho"[52]
That lyte MC was all eyes on this
His eyes mesmerized, by the thighs on this
Homie promised me a chain and that done it
This here was a game – Desi won it. Uh!

*(Dance break. **DESI** shakes her rump and flirts with the **DJ**. She then turns to the audience to say:)*

Y'all can kiss my royal ass[53]

*(**DESI** exits.)* **(BEAT #17 STOPS)**

Scene Nine
The Mart

(ANTIPHOLUS OF EPHESUS enters, hands tied, followed by COP pulling him by the rope like a horse. Spoken.)

COP. Whoa, whoa, that's a good girl! I got some oats for you. Yeah, oats!
I got a certain scratch that needs itchin'
If you catchin' my drift, or maybe you caught a whiff
You understand yet?
I'm gonna go drop the kids off at the pool
I'm gonna go chop a leg off a stool
I'm gonna go fill in the blanks
I'm gonna go make a deposit in the bank
I'm gonna go grow a tail
I'm gonna go give Jonah unto to the whale
I'm gonna go feed the sharks
I'll let two furry creatures float away upon Noah's ark
Are you still in the dark? Let me open your eyes
I've got a wicked fudge monkey on the on-deck circle
I got to take a dump…super size!!!
Super size IT, fat boy – Number 2 with a coke

(COP exits.)

A.E. I gotta get out of here fast, no fakin'
This pig's mind is fried, I swear I'm smellin' bacon
I hope Dromio shows up quick with my bail
Lickety split right quick or I'll end up in jail
Where is he? It's already half past
When da brat gets back I'm gonna kick his funktafied ass[54]

(LUCIANA enters followed by DR. PINCH, a witch doctor who wears a Rastafarian hat and a large tie-die mumu. DR. PINCH carries a woven bag, filled with various bottles and remedies.)

LUC. Dr. Pinch, Dr. Pinch, Dr. Pinch, Dr. Pinch, Dr. Pinch

Oh, Dr. Pinch the situation's wack
My sister's husband tried to get me in the sack
He's gone all crazy and he's on the road, Jack
I don't Kerouac how much just put him back on track
(BEAT #18 STARTS)

DR. P. Hey Luciana, Hey Luciana
So you say yo sistah husband gone banana
Well I can fix him quick if you know that's what you wanna
I say first, put yo hands in the air-ha
Now, wave dem around like you just don't care-ha

LUC. I don't care-ha! I don't care-ha!

DR. P. Say, Rock da nation!

LUC. Rock the nation!

DR. P. Say, Eek-chinacea!

LUC. Eeq-fantasia!

DR. P. DJ, help me out with this one!
Rock da nation, rock da nation
Eek-chinacea, rock, rock da na –
Ooh, taba, taba spoon of herbal cure
Little tiny bottle but a big wonda
Open up me wicker bag and come take look
I got stinky brown stuff in de tiny cups
St. John's Wart, Archibald's too
Nasty toe jelly from inside me shoe
I got St. John's Fungus, I got St. Mary's Bunion
Breath Assure if yo mouth ate the Funyun
This makes you so sunny you tink it Key Largo
An aromatic resin balsum balm bomb bargo
Got a man in bed raising only half mast?
Pinch got a something give him full blast
If you stomach locked I give wheat grass
Have you run real fast with yo hands on yo –
I say, eek-chinacea, rock rock da nation

LUC. Eeq-fantasia, rock the potato?

DR. P. I got anything that grows under da sun
You ask anybody, ask anyone
'Who's the herbal doctor wit all the remedy?'
Dem all point at me, say me name 'Dr. P!'

LUC. Dr. P! Dr. P! Dr. P! Dr. P!
What kind of herbs do you have to help me?

DR. P. Well let me see first tell me what he eat
Someting in his diet maybe make him cheat
Now tell me do he eat veggie or do he eat meat
I say, tell me his diet while we move the feet

LUC. Tell me his diet while we move the feet

DR. P. I say, do not repeat when I say, 'I say'

LUC. Do not repeat when I say, 'I say'

DR. P. Luciana, what is his diet?

LUC. Oh, all he eats is meatloaf –

DR. P.   – dat just might
Dat just might, dat just might be de problem
Troubles in his system, you know I can solve dem
I gotta potent celibacy lotion
Rub his bum make him numb no more sex motion
It got a sauce called Anti-silico-nee
It make him resists de big fat breast dat are phony[55]
I got me worldwide herbal sensation
Put your hands in the air-ha, say eek-chinacea

LUC. Euthenasia, gimme euthenasia

DR. P. I got anything that grows under da sun
You ask anybody, ask anyone
'Who's the herbal doctor wit all the remedy?'
Dem all point at me, say me name 'Dr. P!'

LUC. Dr. P! Dr. P! Dr. P! Dr. P!
Give me three eek-chinacea, no give me three!
Now let's go find him, oh wait there he is
His hands are tied up, can't get easier than this

DR. P. Hurry now, Luciana, get inside my colorful coat
I walk up to him, I move very slow
I make friends with him, you stay below
When I say, 'I say' you pour down da throat

(**LUCIANA** *climbs under* **DR. PINCH**'s *mumu.* **DR. PINCH**, *with the obvious bulge sticking out, crosses to* **ANTIPHOLUS OF EPHESUS**.)

Beaucoup! Hello dere, me friend, nice weather today, eh?
You just stand right dere while I say, 'I say'

(*pause*)

I say, Luciana, jump out of me coat
LUC. (*from under coat*) Luciana, jump out of me coat
DR. P. I say, do not repeat when I say, 'I say'
LUC. Do not repeat when I say, 'I say'
DR. P. Luciana, jump out of my coat! **(MUSIC STOPS)**
LUC. Luciana –
DR. P. (*revealing* **LUCIANA**) – pour de eek-chinecea down his throat

(**LUCIANA** *pours echinacea down* **ANTIPHOLUS**' *throat.*)

A.E. **(MUSIC STARTS)** What the hell are you doing, you crazy sap?
What the hell was that, tastes like elephant crap
DR. P. That's not elephant poop – it's elephant urine
Go ahead, Luciana, let's see if we cure him

(**DR. PINCH** *extends his hands and telepathically starts controlling* **LUCIANA**'s *body movements, causing her to shake and gyrate seductively.*)

DR. P. Shake, shake, sista, shake what yo momma gave ya
See if he still want to be yo little love slave-a
LUC. How you like this, Antipholus?
Do you want a kiss, Antipholus?
Wanna feel the bliss, Antipholus?
Martini with a twist, Antipholus?

(ANTIPHOLUS kicks LUCIANA away from him.)

A.E. Get the hell on, Feluciana[57]
You know I never did and you know I don't wanna
I wouldn't touch your ass with a ten foot staff
Besides, Luciana, you're an ugly giraffe

(LUCIANA stares blankly into space and laughs.)

DR. P. Well, pretty lady, he seem to be cured
He don't want to touch yo stank booty no more

A.E. Hey Lucee, I didn't mean to insult you, I'm sorry
Why don't you and this weird Rastafari
Come untie this rope 'cause it's giving me burns
(aside) Got to get out of here quick before that cop returns

LUC. I'll set you free on one condition
You return home and end Adriana's suspicion
She thinks you love me, we must end her worry

A.E. Okay Luciana, I promise, just hurry

LUC. *(as DR. PINCH removes rope)* C'mon Dr. P, he's almost free
Yay, yippee, Antiph, follow me

A.E. Hell stinky no, I'm free, free at last[58]
Time to go whoop myself some Dromio ass

(ANTIPHOLUS OF EPHESUS exits.)

LUC. But, you promised ...

(LUCIANA exits.)

DR. P. *(to audience)* Hey dere, friendly people, you are all me friends
What you say you put yo hands together and we make amends
Now everybody clap, everybody start clappin'
Hey you in de back, stop nappin'
Hey man ova here with grey hair on ya head
You still pretty old, but, hey, you not dead
Now everybody clap everybody keep clappin
I want both of those hands to be slappin

Girl in tird row, with big balsam boobies[59]
See me after da show I trow you my room keys
Kid with no arms third row from de back
Don't feel bad, you don't have to clap
Now everybody clap, everybody keep clappin
Make some noise for da four guys rappin!
Say Rock da Nation *(Audience: "Rock da Nation")*
Say Eek-chinacea *(Audience: "Eek-chinacea")*
Say Boucoup *(Audience: "Boucoup")*
Put your hands in the air ha…

(COP enters.)

COP. Stop the music! **(MUSIC STOPS)**
Everybody put your hands in the air!

(DR. PINCH pours echinacea down COP's throat.)

And wave 'em around like you just don't care ha!? **(MUSIC STARTS)**

DR. P. Ladies throw your panties and underwear-ha in the air ha[60]
Now wave them around like you just don't care-ha

COP. Damnit, I just don't care ha!

DR. P. I got anything that grows under da sun
You ask anybody, you can ask anyone
'Who's the herbal doctor wit all the remedy?'
Dey all point at me, say me name 'Dr. P!'

COP. Dr. P. Dr. P. Dr. P. Dr. P.

DR. P. Mr. Police Officer please follow me
And say Rock da nation

COP. Rock da nation

DR. P. Say Eek-chinacea

COP. Eek-chinacea

DR. P. I say do not repeat when I say, "I say."

COP. Fine

DR. P. Ha!

(DR. PINCH and POLICEMAN exit.) **(BEAT #18 FADES)**

Scene Ten
Chase Scene

(ANTIPHOLUS OF SYRACUSE enters with duffle bag, stands center stage waiting, and starts beatboxing. DJ comes in with the beat.) **(BEAT #19 STARTS)**

(ADRIANA enters, spots ANTIPHOLUS OF SYRACUSE, and advances on him.)

(ANTIPHOLUS OF SYRACUSE exits with duffle bag – **ADRIANA** *exits, running after him.)*

(DROMIO OF SYRACUSE enters with backpack and boombox.)

D.S. Brother Antipholus, where are you? We gotta catch that plane!

(ANTIPHOLUS OF EPHESUS enters.)

A.E. You're a dead man!

(ANTIPHOLUS charges at DROMIO. COP enters with gun drawn, stopping ANTIPHOLUS OF EPHESUS.)

COP. Freeze!

(ANTIPHOLUS OF EPHESUS turns and exits, running. COP trains the gun on DROMIO OF SYRACUSE.)

Freeze!

(DROMIO OF SYRACUSE exits running.)

(exiting) Damnit! Nobody ever listens to me…

(COP exits. ANTIPHOLUS OF SYRACUSE enters, looks around cautiously, and exits.)

(HENDELBERG enters, crosses stage, exits, screams offstage, re-enters followed by DR. PINCH.)

DR. P. Say Rock the Nation!
HEN. Rock the Nation!
DR. P. Say Eek-chinacea!
HEN. Eek-chinacea!
DR. P. Say it again!

HEN. It again!

(HENDELBERG and DR. PINCH exit.)

*(**ACTOR (2)** dressed as Hendelberg enters, crosses stage, and exits. **MC HENDELBERG** enters, crosses stage, and exits. A stage hand dressed as Hendelberg enters, makes full cross round stage and exits. **ACTOR (1)** dressed as Hendelberg enters and the other three Hendelbergs enter and join hands centerstage. They dance.)*

ALL. Shalomies to my homies, *etc. (join hands, dance)*
Dreidel, dreidel, dreidel, I made it out of clay,
And when it's dry and ready, then dreidel I will play –
Hey!

*(All **HENDELBERGS** exit.)*

*(**LUCIANA** enters, running across stage. **DJ** slows down beat. **LUC** does slow-mo. **DJ** spins the beat backwards and **LUCIANA** runs in slow-mo backwards. **DJ** restores beat. **LUCIANA** runs forward, slams into the set and exits.)*

*(**DROMIO OF SYRACUSE** enters, crosses left, crosses right, sees light on at OPP, crosses right as **ANTIPHOLUS OF EPHESUS** enters and spots him. **DROMIO OF SYRACUSE** goes into OPP.)*

D.S. *(exiting, closing door)* A-B-C ya!

*(**ANTIPHOLUS OF EPHESUS** knocks on OPP door. **DROMIO OF EPHESUS** enters, crosses to **ANTIPHOLUS OF EPHESUS**, and slaps his butt. **ANTIPHOLUS OF EPHESUS** turns to see **DROMIO OF EPHESUS** run into Antipholus of Ephesus' house.)*

D.E. *(exiting, closing door)* D-E-F ya!

*(**ANTIPHOLUS OF EPHESUS** crosses and knocks on Antipholus of Ephesus' House door.)*

A.E. G-H-I'm gonna kick your butt!

*(**DROMIO OF SYRACUSE** enters from OPP.)*

D.S. Brother, you gotta go in there…you gotta go in there! What, man? What?

(**ANTIPHOLUS OF EPHESUS** *chases him offstage, both exit.*)

(**LUCIANA** *enters.* **ACTOR** (**3**) *dressed as Luciana enters. They cross, passing each other and stop, aware that something is odd. They turn to face one another and after a frightened reaction, they laugh, clap, and come to meet each other center stage. They play with each other's hair saying, "Pretty, Pretty!" and then dismiss each other, and exit.*)

(**BOBBY** *the Bike Messenger enters.*)

BOB. My name is Bobby and I'm really cool
I get up early in the morning, and I go to brush my teeth
I like to rap. It is my hobby
If you don't know my name, just call me on my cell phone
I'm a bike messenger, I ride a bike for work
I'm a really nice guy, so don't call me a...

(*Before he can finish, a back-up singer* (**1**), *an actor dressed as Shakespeare* (**4**), *and an Actor* (**3**) *in Luciana dress and gorilla mask and gorilla gloves enter in that order.*)

ALL 3. Ass-hole!![61]

(*They trample* **BOBBY** *and exit.* **BOBBY** *gets up.*)

BOB. (*excited*) Dude, that was a monkey!!

(**BOBBY** *exits. Chase scene ends. Music continues as Church Music is heard in the beat.*)

Scene Eleven
Church and OPP

(DJ CUTS FROM BEAT #19 TO BEAT #20)
*(**DROMIO OF EPHESUS** enters, running.)*

D.E. If my master finds me he's going to deck me
 I need some guardian angels to protect me

*(**DROMIO OF EPHESUS** exits into Church. **ANTIPHOLUS OF EPHESUS** enters, running.)*

A.E. That pig's on my tail, I need a safe haven[62]
 I'll duck into here and say I need savin'

*(**ANTIPHOLUS OF EPHESUS** exits into Church. **LUCIANA** enters.)*

LUC. This way sister, this way
 I saw him run in the church, perhaps to say prayers
 Perhaps to seek penance for all his affairs
 Come on sister, they're almost gone
 Hurry up and put your costume on

*(**ADRIANA** enters putting on her wig and carrying a fake rock [concealed].)*

ADR. When I find my servant I will kick his butt
 And when I find my husband I will give him the what
LUC. The what?
ADR.   For!
LUC.   For what?
ADR.   What for!
LUC.   What for?
ADR. Exactly, now back me while I knock on the door

*(**ADRIANA** knocks on church's door – Church music is heard. **ABBESS (ABB)** opens Church doors and enters. Abbess wears a whistle around her neck like a referee. She speaks like Julie Andrews. A Nerf basketball hoop hangs on the inside of one of the Church's doors.)*

ABB. Hello, children, how are you this eve?

ADR. Oh, kind sister, you wouldn't believe
   What's happened today
ABB.   Speak, child, speak
ADR. All day long my husband's been such a creep
   It started at dinner when he was acting insane
   But before that he promised me this gold chain
   It's hard to explain
ABB.   – Yes, child, do tell

*(**DESI** enters wearing the Chain.)*

DES. Well, well, well, well, well, well, well!
ABB. Desi!
DESI. Sister! *(kiss, kiss)*
   Girl, how you doin?
ABB. Good, how are you sister?
DESI. Girl, what are you in?
ABB. This old thing?
DESI. God must be in love. Hey, how do you like my new club?
ABB. It's beautiful
DESI. Thanks. I gotta go, I gotta customer tha's in love!
ABB. Have fun.
DES. *(to **LUC** & **ADR**)* Freak da funk y'all lookin' at?
   Got beef? Sure 'nuff I'll be cookin' that
   You need to do something with that weave girl

   *(**DESI** exits into OPP.)*

ADR. That slut had my necklace around her throat[63]
   He must have been with her then given her my gold
   My husband's inside, I need to talk to him
   Could you please send him out so I could throw this rock at him?

   *(**ADRIANA** reveals rock.)*

ABB. No, I'm afraid I must make an objection
These men came to me seeking God's protection
(takes rock) There'll be no bloodshed on this sacred ground
That's a technical penalty, please turn around

(**ABBESS** *blows whistle, basketball game ensues.* **ABBESS** *slam-dunks rock into basket over* **ADRIANA** *and* **LUCIANA.** **DJ** *can cut in arena crowd roar noise.*)

ADR. But you don't understand, he's an adulterer

LUC. He cheated on her and insulted her

ABB. Well, if the man's head is too hot, they say
It's 'cause his bed is too cold – Good day

LUC. Oh my God!

(**ABBESS** *exits into church, closing doors.*)

ADR. What do you know about the bedroom, you're a gosh darn nun!

LUC. High five, sister

(**ANTIPHOLUS OF SYRACUSE** *and* **DROMIO OF SYRACUSE** *enter running, carrying their bags.*)

D.S. The airports this way, master, run!

(*All four see each other and scream.* **ANTIPHOLUS OF SYRACUSE** *exits into OPP.*)

ADR. Do my eyes deceive me or is there magic in the air
That somehow they're in here and yet they're over there

LUC. Whoa, this is, like, really, weird

(**DROMIO OF SYRACUSE** *makes a cross sign with his fingers and aims it at the women.*)

D.S. Hssssssss

(**LUCIANA** *screams, holding her eyes in pain, and runs away backwards to the other side of the stage.* **DROMIO** *looks out at the audience and shrugs his shoulders, exits into OPP, closing door.*)

LUC. Owww… it hurts my eyes

ADR. Quick, sister, they're getting away
Let's go capture them, sister, seize the day!

LUC. Yay! Carpe Diem!

(**ADRIANA** and **LUCIANA** exit into OPP. **ABBESS (ABB)** enters through the Church doors. Church music is heard. **ANTIPHOLUS OF EPHESUS** and **DROMIO OF EPHESUS** follow – they have their arms around each other, pretending to be best friends.)

ABB. Well, children, it seems the coast is clear
You can go now but know you're always welcome here

A.E. Thank you very much, sister, now we're done hiding
We'll be on our way, praise the almighty!

ABB. Yes, child, bless you, but do not forget
No fighting between you two children I said
No hurting, name calling, no chasing away
No kicking each other in the balls – Good day[64]

(**ABBESS** exits into church, closing door.)

A.E. I'll tear you to pieces, you can't run for cover

D.E. Just kill me fast and tell Bertha I love her

(They fight as **DROMIO OF SYRACUSE** and **ANTIPHOLUS OF SYRACUSE** enter from OPP.)

D.S. While Adriana and that hooker are having that cat fight[65]
We'll still get out of town and make it out on that flight

A.S. Word, let's be out.

(As **DROMIO OF EPHESUS** frees himself from **ANTIPHOLUS OF EPHESUS**' beating, the other two twins run straight into their respective twin – BAM! They bounce apart and see each other.) **(MUSIC STOPS)**

(The two sets of twins face each other for a few seconds of silence.)

A.E. Wow
A.S. Holy cow
D.E. Holy sheep shit[66]
D.S. Oh my god
A.E. This is odd
A.S. This is deep shit[67]
D.E. Is this true?
D.S. Am I you?
A.E. Are you him?
A.S. Who is he?
D.E. There are two
D.S. Who are you?
A.E. You're my twin
A.S. You are me
D.E. How ya do?
D.S. We're a crew
A.E. Where ya been?
A.S. Who are we?
D.E. You are you
D.S. I am too
A.E. I am him
A.S. It's the key
We have long lost twins, and now we meet
The link's no longer missing
ALL. NOW WE'RE COMPLETE!

(The two **ANTIPHOLI** *and two* **DROMIOS** *hug.)*

A.E. I was angry before but now I'm not
I'm shocked, and this sure explains a whole lot
D.E. For example, why you wanted to kick my ass[68]
D.S. And why my ass did task after task
A.S. And why I received all them golden gifts
A.E. And why MC Hendelberg got so miffed
A.S. And why everyone in town knows me by –
A.S./D.S. – name!

A.E. And why I was arrested and put to such shame
D.E. And why you asked me to have sex with you behind that dumpster[69]

(pause)

D.E. No, I'm just kidding, none of y'all did that
A.E. *(to* **ANTIPHOLUS OF SYRACUSE***)* You didn't…uh…with Adriana?
A.S. No, I didn't wanna
I wanted her sister, Lu-ciana
I wanna make that girl my baby momma
A.E. Now I see why my wife had strayed from me
A.S. And why Luciana runs away from me
There both in there and they're downstairs
Let's go explain that this has been a comedy of errors
A.E. Lead and I will follow, my newfound brother
A.S. Nay, pound for pound, not one before the other

*(***ANTIPHOLUS OF SYRACUSE** *and* **ANTIPHOLUS OF EPHESUS** *hug, then exit into OPP as* **DROMIO OF SYRACUSE** *opens and closes door for them. Then* **DROMIO OF SYRACUSE** *crosses to* **DROMIO OF EPHESUS***, excitedly.)*

D.S. What's your name?
D.E. Dromio. What's your name?
D.S. Dromio

(They grin at each other, then, slowly at first…)

D/D. *(dancing)* -io, oh-oh-io,
Oh io, oh-oh-io,
Oh io, oh-oh-io,
Come on, everybody, do the baseball!
(hugging) What! What's that about son! What's that all about!

(They separate and immediately start doing a mirror exercise, mirroring each other's moves exactly. They try to psych the other out, surprising them with a move, but the other mirrors perfectly.)

D/D. Whoa…whoa….whoa…woo bam!
 I knew you were gonna do that. I totally did

   (*The* **DROMIOS** *sit down on the ground and play patty cake as* **ABBESS** *enters from church with bubbles.*)

ABB. It's eight o'clock time to blow friendly bubbles

   (**ABBESS** *blows bubbles. Then she sees the* **DROMIOS**.)

   Oh, my God, am I seeing double?

D.S. Do you like cheese?
D.E.   Yeah
D.S.   Me too
D.E. What's your favorite color?
D/D.   Blue!
ABB. (*singing, operatic, a capella*) There's some magic in the wind
   The gentle voices of these twins
   Shoots me back to years ago
   When life was tough and tears would flow
   But now methinks I'm filled with joy
   For I have found my long lost boys
   (*speaking*) Excuse me, children, who look the same
   Might I ask of you your name?
D/D. Dromio
ABB.   – io, Oh-io, Oh-oh-io,
   Come on, everybody do the baseball!
   Now I know, the truth has finally been discovered
   Dromios
D/D.   Yeah?
ABB.   I am your mother!
D.E. What?
ABB.   Yes it's me, your mother, Betty
   I was so very young and I just wasn't ready
   To raise you alone after your father died
   So I fled to a sports nunnery far away to hide
   Everyone thought I had committed suicide
   Oh how I've cried, oh how I've cried

D/D. Mom!

ABB. But I knew we would meet, I've been waiting for this
Where's Antipholus and Antipholus?

D.S. They're just inside the whorehouse[70]

ABB. Yes, well, right, well I won't be a bore now and ruin their fun
Besides, that's not the place for introductions
I've dreamt of this moment, we're finally together
And I'll be your mother forever and ever[71]

(**ABBESS** *exits into church followed by* **DROMIO OF EPHESUS**. **DROMIO OF SYRACUSE** *closes door behind them and addresses audience.*)

D.S. So, Antipholus has Luciana. The other Antipholus has Adriana and Dromio's got Bertha. The DJ's got Desi. So...
I'll be mingling about after the show...

(**DROMIO OF SYRACUSE** *exits into church.*) (**DJ** *puts on the last section of* **BEAT #20** *with the drums only, underscoring the scene*) (**ANTIPHOLUS OF SYRACUSE** *and* **LUCIANA**, *hand in hand enter from OPP. Spoken.*)

LUC. So you're not Antipholus?

A.S. I am Antipholus, Luciana. Come on

LUC. Oh, so he's not Antipholus?

A.S. No, I told you, we're both Antipholus. There's two of us. We're identical twins

LUC. *(slight pause)* Am I Antipholus?

(**ANTIPHOLUS OF SYRACUSE** *and* **LUCIANA** *exit into church.* **ADRIANA** *and* **DESI** *enter from OPP,* **DESI** *holding the Chain.*)

DESI. Well, sister, I guess this rightfully belongs to you

(**DESI** *holds out Chain and* **ADRIANA** *takes it.*)

ADR. Oh, I don't know Desi, it looks so good on you

DESI. Come on now, sister, you keep it

ADR. Well, I think –

DESI. Ok, gimme that

(**DESI** *grabs Chain and exits into OPP, leaving a bewildered* **ADRIANA**. **ADRIANA** *follows into OPP, closing door behind.*)

(**ANTIPHOLUS OF SYRACUSE** *and* **LUCIANA** *enter from the church.* **LUCIANA** *is in a veil with a bouquet of flowers and is singing the Wedding March.*)

LUC. OK, catch

(**LUCIANA** *attempts to throw her wedding bouquet into the house, but ends up tossing it to DJ.*)

LUC. Can we have a pony and name her Gwendolyn?
A.S. You like ponies?
LUC. Yeah – I like riding on top of things[72]
A.S. YEAH!

(**ANTIPHOLUS OF SYRACUSE** *and* **LUCIANA** *exit into Antipholus of Ephesus' House.* **ACTOR** (2) *half emerges from OPP door in Adriana wig, but wearing Antipholus of Ephesus' jacket.*)

ADR. Oh, honey, I'm really sorry about everything

(**ACTOR** *disappears behind door, removes wig, re-emerges.*)

A.E. It's OK, honey, I forgive you

(**ACTOR** *makes out with wig, exits, closing door.*) (**BEAT #20 FADES**)

(*The two* **DROMIOS** *enter from Church, shutting doors as they enter.*)

D.E./D.S. Brother, brother, brother, what a day!
D.S. We found our brothers, our mother's okay
D.E. Our masters are happy and busy romancin'
Hey, I never realized I was so handsome

(*They point at each other, gesturing, "This guy…what a comedian."*)

D.S. Hey, you know that girl Luciana?
D.E. Yeah, that girl's hot
D.S. No, she's not

D.E. She ain't?

D.S. She's dumb as paint
(singing the song) Luciana… hoochy-mamma

D.E. No, no, no, you know who's ugly? Desi.

D.S. Stop yourself, Desi is classy

D.E. Nah – she butt-nasty[73]
I mean she do have much ass, but she also do got a mustache

*(Pause. Both **DROMIOS**, upset, turn away from each other. Beat. They break, turn back and slap hands, smiling.)*

D.E/D.S. Alright – They both fly

D.E. Come on, all is forgiven

D.S. The sun has set and the moon has risen

D.E. Now let's go bust some rhymes, tour about the land

D.S. Maybe start a band

D.E. And enter a new life hand in hand

(BEAT #21 STARTS)

D.E./D.S. Hand in hand. Hand in hand. Hand in hand. Hand in hand….

(blackout)

ALL. Throw your hands up *(x8)*

*(Lights up. **ALL FOUR ACTORS (1, 2, 3, 4)** are now onstage.)*

ALL. Throw your hands up *(x4)*

4. All the people in the back throw your hands up

2. Everybody on this side throw your hands up

3. Everybody on this side throw your hands up

1. If you love your momma throw your hands up

*(Each then gets four lines of freestyle in following order: **(4), (1), (2), (3)**. When the freestyle is over they return to the script:)*

4. The four young brothers were together at last

1. And they shook and they rocked every spot on the map

3. And the audiences clapped and the ladies all screamed
2. And the four young brothers lived out their dream
(BEAT #21 STOPS)
ALL. Thus ends the tale of the Bomb-itty
Thirty years later in {New York} City

(NOTE: Substitute whatever city play is performed in.)

(blackout)

(As actors come up for curtain call, **DJ** *can put* **BEAT #21** *back on)*

ALTERNATE LINES

We think *The Bomb-itty of Errors* is a play that can be performed and enjoyed by people young and old. To that end, we offer some alternate lines here that may appeal to a broader audience.

1. So he turned to a life of crime and greed
   Just to try and get by and give his family what they need
   He took heed to work with people that he trusted
   But it wasn't too long before M.C. E got busted
2. As we flyin' in, you know we smile-a-lin
   Two fresh brothers that be style-a-lin'
3. So for now I'll eat, maybe hit the street
   And scope for some bitties that I wanna meet
   Try out pick up lines, like you sure is sweet
   And see if I can find a girl who likes to freak –
4. What the heck are you doing, for God's sake, peace
5. Nope!
6. 'Cause on the streets they lookin' sly
   You got sorcerers on corners who can slide inside your head
   Scary dudes in shadows that are wishin' that you're dead
   Cheaters, cons, pranksters, mafiosos
   Dealers, punks, gangsters – where did Dro go?
7. What if you were married and wore a rock?
   I would lie in bed and stroke my husband's con –
   fidence, we would laugh and sigh
8. I'd stand in the doorway, undressed, and wait
9. I have no mistress, wife, no attraction
   It's been seven months since I got any action!
10. But sister, you're such a hotty
    Sister, just give him your body
11. But sister, I've still got some perk
    And sister, I'm going berserk
    'Cause my husband's a jerk and I'm starting to cry

12. No way, sister
13. - that your breath is so bad
    It's his own damn fault and it's time to get mad
14. Cut your jokin' kid, what you smokin' kid?
15. You stinky weasel, your brain cells are gone
    As we bounce from town to town, from dusk till dawn
16. CUT LINE
17. CUT LINE
18. Tear the skin from my tainted brow
19. This unknown pair of mistresses
20. Pray, what kinda trash did you splash and spray?
21. Instigate, emulate, consumate, saturate
22. 'Cause you are so lazy
    Walkin' round in a haze countin' daisies, it's crazy
    I don't know if you're dumb or been hittin' the bottle
    You're so stupid you make Luciana look like Aristotle
23. You'd open that door and get the heck out my house
24. Note: Con Edison is a New York City electric company – you should rewrite the line to make sense and rhyme with your local electric company
25. Where for a few evil g's they'll do what you please'll
26. Lu can I fall in love with you?
27. Let's face it, you're a hotty with a sexy body
28. Not mad, try glad. But mad? No no
29. She wanted some and there was nowhere to run!
30. Now I'm treated like a bass ale stout, slurpling' on me
31. Smothering my body and bitin' on my lip
32. – get out of my arms.
33. Now you're wrapped up in a big fat mess
    With some big fat lass in some big fat dress
    With a big fat chest who wants to scream big fat yes!
34. I gotta get out of here before that guy comes back
35. That no good, good-for-nothing, skanky mutt *(D.S. Mutt!)*

36. Get a mic and a cord and a big fat amp
37. I didn't smoke pot, I didn't smoke crack
38. **HEN.** Just to make him a special bling bling
    A.E. Which I never saw in my life
    HEN. To hang around the neck of some ding-aling
39. Mammen's the warden, he's a tough Irish lad
    He'll kill you for sport if you make him mad
    So start reading up on your Gaelic and collecting four leaf clover
    And when you take a shower, avoid bending over
40. I'll blow out your brains if you rag on my stallion
41. He praised your speech? What did he say?
42. Asks you bout something that they said they showed you
43. (*passing money to A.S.*) Here's the cheese and the one time fee
44. Dromio, get out of here!
45. Heck no! But I found it
46. And suddenly I'm lifted, flyin in the sky
47. Miss? Kiss my butt baby
    Save that sweet-talkin' for some other fly lady
48. Well, you got all the trouble, ace
    Give it up or I'm gonna smack up your adorable face
49. This about that sweet, sweet chain you promised me child
50. And competitors are metaphors for that head of yours
51. I caught his eyes looking down my blouse
    He was talkin' bout his ugly spouse
52. But he's a wuss like that, I told him check
    "Gotta what yo, gotta get a roughneck"
53. Y'all can kiss my royal butt
54. It's already half-past, where is that chump?
    When da brat gets back I'm gonna kick his funktafied rump
55. It make him resists de bosoms dat are phony

56. Get out of my face, Feluciana
    You know I never did and you know I don't wanna
    I wouldn't touch you with a 10 foot staff
57. No freakin' way, I'm free, free at last
    Time to find Dromio and break him in half
58. Girl in tird row, with eyes big like rubies
59. Ladies throw hotel keys and underwear-ha
60. Moron!!
61. That cop's on my tail, I need a safe haven
62. That trick had my necklace around her throat
63. No kneeing each other in the groin – Good day
64. While Adriana and that lady are having that cat fight
65. Holy sheep poop
66. This is deep poop
67. For example, why you wanted to tear me apart
    And why I went all over the Mart
68. And why you asked me to give you that erotic massage behind that dumpster
69. They're just inside the brothel
70. *(If the two actors playing Dromio are not the same race)*
    Come, children, follow me, brother and brother
    And I'll explain to you both why you're not the same color
71. Yeah – did I mention I'm a contortionist?
72. Nah – she nasty.
    I mean she do have much sass, but she also do got a mustache

Below is a picture of the original set of the three houses and masking flats.

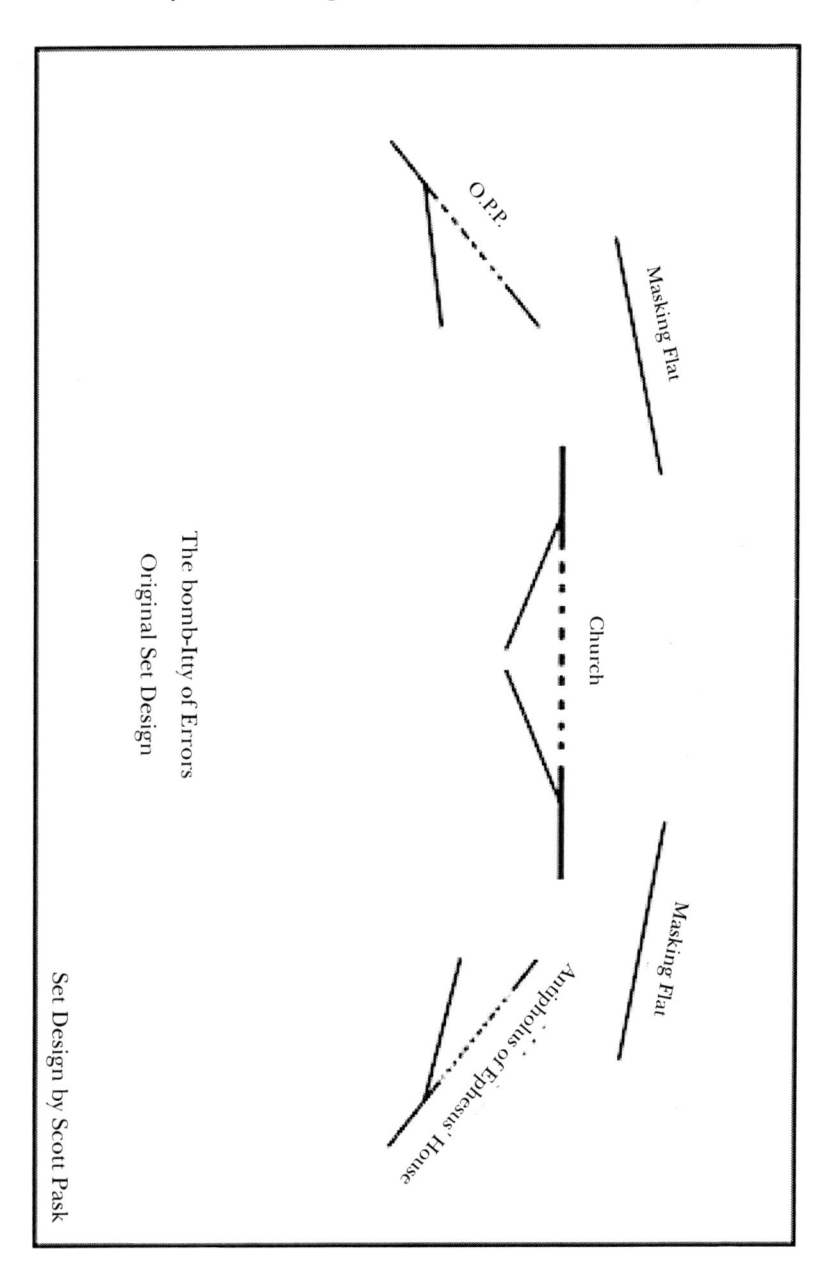

O.P.P.

Masking Flat

Church

The bomb-Itty of Errors
Original Set Design

Masking Flat

Antipholus of Ephesus House

Set Design by Scott Pask

OTHER TITLES AVAILABLE FROM SAMUEL FRENCH

THE PEOPLE VS. FRIAR LAURENCE: THE MAN WHO KILLED ROMEO AND JULIET

Ron West and Phil Swann

Musical Comedy / 6m, 3f / Simple set

A musical comedy spoof starring the Friar of Shakespeare's Romeo and Juliet! Friar Laurence is behind bars, charged for the 'murder' of the lovers. As the trial progresses, mayhem and silliness abound with bits, songs, and scenes equal parts Vaudeville and Bard. A "load of laughs" (*Chicago Sun Times*, highly recommended), *The People Vs. Friar Laurence: The Man who Killed Romeo and Juliet* is sure to leave both Shakespeare scholars and low-brow humorists rolling in the aisles!

"Hysterical—West and Swann have shrouded the tale with witty story devices and a bright cloak of catchy songs that add to the ribald humor while moving the story along in the best traditions of musical theatre."
—*Chicago Sun Times*

SAMUELFRENCH.COM

Breinigsville, PA USA
29 December 2010
252339BV00003B/1/P